THE ART of DYING

Erin Dunham

PublishAmerica
Baltimore

© 2010 by Erin Dunham
All rights reserved. No part of this book may be reproduced, stored in a retrieval system or transmitted in any form or by any means without the prior written permission of the publishers, except by a reviewer who may quote brief passages in a review to be printed in a newspaper, magazine or journal.

First printing

This is a work of fiction. Names, characters, places, and incidents either are the product of the author's imagination or are used fictitiously. Any resemblance to actual persons, living or dead, events, or locales is entirely coincidental.

PublishAmerica has allowed this work to remain exactly as the author intended, verbatim, without editorial input.

Hardcover 978-1-4560-1922-8
Softcover 978-1-4560-1923-5
PUBLISHED BY PUBLISHAMERICA, LLLP
www.publishamerica.com
Baltimore

Printed in the United States of America

For All of You

Terri,
Thank you for
your support.
Good luck with
that guy you bring around...
seriously.
eri

Thank you G.P. for your excitement at the start.
Thank you S.C. for your encouragement and input throughout.
Thank you R.S. for your support this past year.

It was a cool breeze that woke her with a chill. She opened her eyes and admired the white blossoms slowly falling from the branches above her and leisurely floating down to her resting spot; it reminded her of a snowfall. She listened to the sound of the leaves bouncing off of each other from the wind. The cold air irritated Marie enough to get her to sit up and put her sweater on. She looked around a little dazed still from the sleep and she stood up to wipe the blossoms from her white dress.

Marie, when she realized that she was standing a few feet from the edge, felt her heart pound in her chest; the beating resonated in her ears. She took a few small steps closer to the edge of the cliff and leaned to look down over it. She couldn't see the bottom so she edged a little closer still. With her right foot lagging behind her to keep its distance she moved her left leg to the cliff's end and looked over to see the bottom. She was sweating with fear but she enjoyed this feeling of life pumping through her; it had been too long since she had been scared. Her right foot slowly joined its partner on the end of the rock.

She stood very still and held out her arms and closed her eyes, she felt high with adrenaline. As she calmed, her eyes opened again and she lowered her arms feeling more at peace with herself.

She turned to walk back to her white tree when a squirrel ran out onto the rock and startled her. She stepped back but there was no ground under her feet.

She fell.

Her body scraping against the sharp rock as she desperately reached her arms out to stop herself from plummeting. She stopped. Her feet touched down on a piece of rock sticking out from the cliff and her hands were hanging on to a ridge where she had been standing mere seconds before. She screamed and it echoed through the valley but there was no one there to hear it.

Marie gripped on as hard as she could but she knew she didn't have the strength to do it for very long. She took a minute to catch her breath before the tears started streaming down her face. "I can't die like this" she said to herself, "I can't die like this, I can't die like this, I can't die like this."

*K*ay shuffled across her peeling linoleum floor with two tea cups and saucers in her hands, her dirty pink slipper catching on one of the faux tiles. She handed the cup in her left hand to the perky young girl who sat anxiously at her kitchen table and placed the other before her on the table. As Kay sat in the wooden chair across from the girl she noticed her fiddling with a string in her hand, winding it between her fingers and then pulling it out and repeating the action. The centenarian placed her cold wrinkled hand on the girls and asked her to slowdown, took the string and hid it in the pocket of her yellow housecoat. The girl stopped fiddling but mere seconds later her leg started to vibrate the floor.

"So why don't you continue with what you were saying, I am listening now that I have my tea", the elder lady assured her.

"Like I was saying, have you ever felt that a song was written for you? Not like everyone thinks that a song was written for them but in the way that, if the composer ever met you, they would declare to the world, my song was written for you. I have approximately two hundred absolute favorite songs, everyone which, if the composer ever met me they would declare was written for me. In fact, when they make a movie about me, I have already handpicked the soundtrack for every major situation in my life….really, I have thought about this at length. I will most likely make a cameo in the film, if I am too old to play myself."

Kay looked blankly at the girl for a moment before saying, "I, like you, believed in some small way that the world positively revolved around me. It revolved around *me because I was someday going to change it drastically. As of yet I am unsure how it is that I was going to change the world…..but inherently I knew this to be true. It wasn't until I was much older than you that I stumbled upon the reality that this is, at one point in a person's life or another, a notion that the majority of the world believes. I was competing with a large majority of our sweet planet earth's inhabitants to change the world; my next realization was that I was buggered. I looked at myself in the mirror after thirty five years of life and broke the bad news: "you aren't what you thought you were. You think that you are very different from the rest of the world, which is false. In actuality you are more like everyone than you can imagine, the chances are that you will NOT make a difference in the world, in fact you will most likely not even effect another person beyond your close knit group of friends and family. You will not be written about in textbooks nor will you ever publish a book that will outlive you. You are, as nicely as I can put it, just another person in the world that will eke through life and die, being remembered by those closest to you until they pass on. I am sorry I had to be the one to tell you, but this is the way it is."*

The girl quickly responded as she shook her head, "But when I think ahead to my future nothing seems very appealing when I have to be realistic. I am completely against a 'nine to five' job; my mom has worked everyday for forty something years and she is no better for it. My next option is something along the lines of shift work; most shift work involves some sort of manual labor which, believe it or not, I am not a huge fan of. I can always resort to the one thing I am good at, serving; but frankly, I am growing tired of that job. So the only thing left really is to change the world. Here I am back at square one."

Kay smiled condescendingly, "You need to remember what I told you, it's unachievable, unrealistic and far too competitive. The important question then comes into play; why are you here and what are you supposed to do while you are here? Oh Lord, what to do? You will find yourself, at times, feeling far too confident in the decision making skills of a coin."

"At this point I will go anywhere for an answer."

The elder woman took a sip from her tea, set the cup perfectly back on her saucer "don't worry dear, the answer will find you."

James stood outside the funeral home, neither pensive nor thoughtless, blankly trying to expect something. He wiped his damp cheek, decided not to enter and turned towards his red Cavalier for an escape but, just before he took his first step, he was spotted.

Jane was walking out of the red brick building of depression and lit a smoke before the door had time to close. He walked towards her and she smirked at his appearance, his suit was wrinkled and his shirt half tucked in.

"People were starting to wonder if you would show up" she said to him with no empathy what so ever.

"I'm here," he said, "just contemplating whether to go in or not."

"You should pay your respect," she let out as she exhaled her smoke.

James looked down at Jane, she had the body of a runway model minus the height, beautiful long blond hair, and the face of a china doll. He replied to her cold demeanor, "Yeah, her family, you're right, I have to pay my respect".

"I'll see you in there then, it won't be long before this is all over, don't worry" Jane said recognizing that they shared this loss.

James went for the door handle and wondered why Jane seemed so calm and unaffected; Jane wondered how he could be so inconsiderate, but the two of them never really did understand each other. He gave her a nod and walked into the poorly lit hallway. He read the name on a sign and felt faint; her name on the sign meant it was true, she was gone.

He entered the space to which he was directed and took note of the attendants. There were many people he didn't recognize. He did see her brothers laughing to each other in a corner and he was sure they were laughing at her expense; she would love that. Her friends were feeling sorry for themselves in a circle competing for the title of who was closest to her.

Lillian saw him come in and approached him. They didn't say anything to each other; she just pointed him in the direction of Marie's mother. Katherine was less a human figure than a pile of dirty laundry waiting to be dealt with. With her closest friend June by her side, she sat there staring at nothing, she wasn't crying at that moment but she certainly had been. He wondered if she was drunk. When she looked up to see that James had approached her Katherine stood and enveloped his figure as she wept hysterically. It took a few minutes before she could compose sensible words, "where have you been?"

"I just needed time to get here", he told her.

"You sound like Marie. I would have been angry with her", she said with a tone that he had grown accustomed to.

"I know, I am sorry, but I'm here now."

"You are." Katherine pointed to the right, "She is in that room there. I haven't been in yet. You don't have to go in either."

"I better go in, you know that she is watching me and wants to see my reaction."

"That's true" Katherine said with a phony smile "she would love to be here today, quietly judging us and our reactions." Tears fell from her eyes again and she wept aloud.

"Well, I better give her a show then" he said with false enthusiasm.

James kissed Katherine on the cheek, helped her sit back down in her seat and turned towards the entrance to the corpse room. He shut his eyes and took two steps forward to where he knew he would be able to see her.

He opened his eyes. Nausea. Denial. Misery. Relief. There she was.

He approached the casket but held his breath as he took the steps. He knelt before her for the second time. James looked at her face; it wasn't her. This thing in front of him was wearing so much make up and was barely recognizable as a human. The face of this corpse was marred; hers was perfect. He looked down and noticed that this imposter was wearing Marie's gown; her mother must have picked it out. He remembered admiring her figure in the dress as he would spin her around when they danced. His head dropped and he wept.

The aroma of lilacs surrounded him; he took a few deep breaths to calm himself down but the scent merely encouraged hysterics. She couldn't have had a more appropriate flower on her casket, lilacs were her favorite. The almost overbearing scent reminded him of a time before all of this.

James turned the key inside the lock to open the front door. As he pushed the door away from him an aroma met him as he entered. Down the hallway he could see a bouquet of white flowers on a table where a lamp used to sit. He kicked off his shoes and walked down the hall.

"Honey, are you here? Great flowers, they smell beautiful." He spoke loudly not knowing exactly where she was.

As he turned the corner he noticed another white arrangement on the television; there was a purple bunch on the dining table. Walking into the kitchen he picked up a vase off the floor that was filled with the same flower and set it on the counter beside some darker colored cuttings of the bloom. He shook his head and took a deep breath.

"Are you here?" He yelled, "where'd you get these flowers from?"

He slid into the bathroom to discover yet another bunch in an old wine bottle. He admired them while he emptied his bladder. As he zipped back up he yelled out,

"I know you're here I can hear the music on!"

He snuck into the bedroom with the intention of scaring Marie but was disappointed to find three flower arrangements in her place. Before he had time to figure out where she could be the front door burst open. He walked out to greet her and laughed out loud upon the sight of her. She was struggling to get her keys out of the door with so many flowers in her arms that he thought she might fall over from the sheer weight.

Still laughing at the hilarity of this bazaar situation he found it in himself to ask,

"What's up with the flowers?"

"Aren't they beautiful?" She asked, begging for encouragement.

"Yes but what's up with them?" He repeated his inquiry.

"I can't say that I know what you mean by that", she said honestly. "God it smells amazing in here. Don't you think?"

Marie made her way into the kitchen, her pruning area, and began to sort the blossoms. James followed her and continued, "There are a lot of flowers in the apartment. What's up with that?"

"They are lilacs, not flowers, and what do you mean?"

"Why are there so many?" he asked.

"Because lilacs are one of my favorite things in the world and we don't get enough time with them so I want to spend what little time I can with them in excess."

"Okay….but.."

"Don't they smell unbelievable?" She asked again, cutting him off.

"Yeah…but.."

"Did you know that, unlike other flowers, the scent of a lilac can travel; with a nice breeze I bet it could go as far as a mile."

"That's nice but…." James started, but Marie was moving at a much faster pace as she cut him off.

"Lilacs are elegant…like a rose, you know? A bride could absolutely carry a bouquet of lilacs proudly down the aisle. But they aren't pretentious like a rose….no, they're easy going like a daisy, but without the simplicity….you know?"

"What are you talking about?" James asked with frustration, "Can you hear yourself? Where'd these flowers come from?"

"The church", she replied.

"The church gave you all these flowers?" he asked curiously.

"Not exactly. They have all those bushes on their property and I just went over and cut these ones off", she explained.

"Let me clarify here…you stole these flowers from the church?"

"Relax….if the priest knew how much I adore lilacs he wouldn't have a problem with me taking some. I would have asked but there was a mass

THE ART OF DYING

in progress and besides, I just knew it would be alright." She was assuring him because she could sense the stress in his voice.

"Okay, so you stole from the church while they were most likely preaching against sin...that's super."

James left the kitchen and stormed to the bedroom; he sat at the desk and thought to himself. He rationalized that, since she didn't get caught and there was no harm done, he wouldn't get mad about this. He wondered if she actually thought that her actions were acceptable. After calming himself, he walked back to her in the kitchen. He noticed that she was wearing lilacs in her hair. He adored it when she put flowers between her locks.

"Do you not see anything wrong with what you did?" he asked her as a parent would ask their child.

"Of course not, why? Do you?"

"No, I was just wondering."

"Grab me those scissors please", she said with her hand out waiting for him to help her.

He handed Marie the scissors and watched as she beautifully arranged three more works of art, using lilacs as her medium. James continued to watch her and how oblivious she was that he was in the room. He wondered what the attachment was to these flowers but didn't ask; he had learned that some things were only for her. She sang to herself and even took a moment to roll around on the floor with one of the cats. He witnessed her as she whole heartedly embraced one of her filled vases while absorbing their beauty with her senses; she was in heaven then and he knew it.

I cannot believe that I am here right now and that you are gone, he thought, still on his knees beside the open casket. He raised his head to look at her pale face. *What have you done?*

Why now and why like this? James reached out to rip off a small cluster of white flowers from the lilacs that hung the closest to her body. He brought them to his nose and inhaled. James knew that the smell of a flower would never haunt a man as the aroma of a lilac would destroy him in years to come. It occurred to him; this was a part of her plan. He smiled to himself with curiosity of things to come before he stood, and walked away. Though he said nothing to anyone as he left, most people noticed him go. He waited outside chain smoking until it was his time to speak.

Samson was sitting in the funeral home listening to a circle of dismal females compare Marie stories to determine, what appeared to be, who was the closest to the deceased. He noticed James enter the room and look around searchingly but James approached Marie's mother before he could get up to greet him. He sat back down and wondered why he had come at all.

His eyes were constantly drawn to Marie's brothers in the corner who didn't have the utmost respect for the dead. They were laughing out loud and joking about their sister and some stupid things that she had done. Samson was surprised no one had said anything to them, maybe he would; maybe not. Connor stood out from the bunch as the only man in the place wearing jeans and, unlike the majority of his Arian looking siblings, he had dark, afro like hair with an unkempt beard to match. He was the loudest of the four boys, his laugh was very distinct.

Samson thought that if Marie was here that she would stop them from shooting their mouths off; maybe she wouldn't, she was hard to predict.

He thought of how he met her, their common interest was literature; they were sitting beside each other at a bar. She appeared completely interested in his every word but he knew somehow that she was completely uninterested in him personally. This is how they remained friends he decided: his acknowledgment of her disinterest. She very rarely talked about their personal lives but he could remember the last time they met when she had.

Samson sat across from Marie at the pub; he was the only friend she had that could talk about books and such for hours on end without attempting to change the subject to more personal matters. He had inquired numerous times about her mood; he knew that something was bothering her. After a length of silence wherein she was clearly trying to organize her thoughts, she blurted out, "Why is it that, as you age, the world seems more difficult to bear? It is ridiculous."

"Well that seems a little negative Marie. And I don't really understand the context".

"What am I talking about? I don't know. What I mean is, well, I don't know, it's weird."

"Just say whatever you think you mean then."

"I mean, I wish I could figure things out", she said with frustration.

"Figure what out?"

"The world I guess. Figure out why."

"I can't say that I am following you completely." Samson laughed at her broken thoughts, "why what?"

"Why anything", she replied.

"Yeah, okay…what then, what after you figure out why?"

"Um….well, then I could make a plan I guess"

"Okay, now we might be getting somewhere, a plan for what?" he inquired.

"I guess like a plan for greatness or something, to help people, to help myself, to be remembered, pass on a legacy".

"Well, I wish you luck on that endeavor. I must say though that I think you are stressing out a little too much about this."

"Do I sound nuts?" she asked laughing as she took a sip from her Guinness.

"You would to someone getting to know you. Lucky for us I already know you are nuts so this is no shock to me." The two held their glasses up and gave cheers to his honesty.

"Sometimes I think you should spend less time yapping and more time shutting up", she said maintaining her smile.

"I will shut up about your insanity but not about that Umberto Eco book you leant me; what did you think?"

"I thought the main character and I shared some spectacular qualities."

"As well as a major flaw I suppose." The two of them gave another cheers and laughed while they continued yet another novel conversation.

Samson stood from his seat when he noticed Theresa come into the reception area. She was wearing red, an odd choice he thought to himself but who was he to comment on fashion or inappropriateness. When she saw him the two embraced and she asked, "How long have you been here?"

"About half an hour. It has been pretty lonely though, James came and left without a word and I don't think she made any friends in University aside from the two of us."

Theresa smiled and agreed, "Isn't that the truth? She never was much of a fan of people."

"Yes, well, let's take it easy on her for today", Samson said protectively.

"Fair enough", she agreed. "Have you been in to see her?"

"Don't think I will be doing that, I know how I want to remember her and it is not as a corpse."

"So you're scared are you?" she teased him.

"Well for Christ's sake, it's creepy." Samson acted as if he could joke about things though it killed him to act so detached.

"I think she would love to watch you squirm" Theresa continued joking with him.

"It's not happening."

"Fine then, let's have a seat."

The pair sat beside one another and thought to themselves for a moment. The silence was tormenting Samson and so, he broke it,

"When did you see her last?"

"Oh, I don't know we have been pretty busy since we graduated. We had lunch about six months ago"

"Did she seem weird at all?" He asked, hoping to solve what he thought to be a mysterious death.

"No, she was her normal peculiar self, why?"

"Just wondering."

They sat pensively for a few minutes, each of them recalling aspects of their dead friend. Samson shed a tear despite his best efforts not to; Theresa laughed out loud.

"I would rather be thinking about what you are remembering" he said.

"I was just thinking about a class that we had together, I forget what the topic was exactly, maybe *The Novel*. It was just so typical Marie."

Theresa took comfort in the memory as she hadn't seen her friend in a very long time.

The professor handed back some papers and made eye contact with Marie as she came in late. "You made it today Marie, and you only managed to miss more than half the class."

"Sorry Professor Gilmour, I…."

"I'm sure I have heard it before, here's your paper." The professor turned to the class and said "If anyone has any questions about or problems with their marks then see me after class in my office."

The tardy student took her place beside Theresa, removed her sweater and took out her notebook and pen. The perfectly figured young professor made her way back up to the podium to continue her lecture. Marie turned over her paper to see an 80% marked in red with some commentary. *Not bad*, she thought to herself, *for a rush job*.

She took her pen in hand and began to make notes as the professor continued, "Flaubert uses irony to criticize romanticism and to investigate the relation of beauty to corruption and of fate to free will. Emma embarks directly down a path to moral and financial ruin over the course of the novel. She is very beautiful, as we can tell by the way several men fall in love with her, but she is morally corrupt and unable to accept and appreciate the realities of her life. Since her childhood she has read novels that feed her discontent with her ordinary life. She dreams of the purest, most impossible forms of love and wealth, ignoring whatever beauty is present in the world around her."

She continued, "Flaubert once said, 'Madame Bovary is me,' and many scholars believe that he was referring to a weakness he shared with his character for romance, sentimental flights of fancy, and melancholy. Flaubert, however, approaches romanticism with self-conscious irony, pointing out its flaws even as he is tempted by it. Emma, on the other hand, never recognizes that her desires are unreasonable. She rails emotionally against the society that, from her perspective, makes her desires impossible to achieve. Does anyone have any questions so far? Yes ...Chris."

The class turned towards the back of the room and listened to their fellow classmate ask, "Is it possible that Flaubert didn't write an unappreciative greedy woman but rather a character with what we would now consider a disorder of some kind? I mean...he probably based this character on someone right? It just seems like, even if it was based on himself, that this person had some serious mental problems; she is, at times, completely separated from reality."

"Well, as my lecture continues I will reveal my opinion for the most part. Why don't I continue and then I will readdress your question at the end?"

"Okay" he agreed.

"Are there any other questions?...No? Moving on. Emma's failure is not completely her own. Her character reflects the many ways in which circumstance, rather than free will, determined the position of a woman. We can see that Emma's role as a woman may have an even greater effect on the course of her life than her social status does. Emma is frequently portrayed as the object of a man's gaze. But Emma's inability to accept her situation and her attempt to escape it through adultery and deception constitute moral errors. These mistakes bring about her ruin and, in the process, cause harm to innocent people around her. For example, though dim-witted and unable to recognize his wife's true character, Charles loves Emma, and she deceives him. He ends up dying as a result of Emma's selfish spending and suicide. Yes Marie, do you have a question or are you just scratching?"

"I have a question", Marie replied.

"Go ahead."

Marie gazed quickly down at the almost blank piece of paper in front of her. She reread the sentence she just wrote down to be sure she had it right.

"The last thing you said was 'He ends up dying as a result of Emma's selfish spending and suicide'. Are you saying that her spending was selfish or that her spending and her suicide were selfish?"

"Well both of course, but I am not sure what relevance that has to the lecture."

"So you are saying that her suicide was selfish?" Marie clarified.

"I am." Professor Gilmour agreed, "she killed herself because she ran up an enormous debt and then when she couldn't whore herself out of it the only other solution she considered was to kill herself; an easy way out that actually resulted in her husband's death and her daughter becoming an orphan. Yes, I think that this was a selfish choice on her behalf."

"What if Chris is right and Emma is based on someone who had a mental disorder or suffered from depression or what if she was killing herself in order to solve her problems as well as the problems of others?"

"Well she didn't. She was just a selfish woman who wanted the world, continuously changed her mind, and went through periods of betrayal and then guilt according to her actions."

"Interesting that someone so smart could be so ignorant", Marie let out under her breath.

"Excuse me", the professor said trying to contain her anger.

"I meant Emma Bovary" the student said to cover her off handed comment.

"Of course you did."

Marie smiled to herself complacently. Theresa noticed her friend's expression and laughed out loud. As the professor tried to collect her thoughts to continue the lecture, she noticed the time on her watch. A few people in the class began to pack up their books.

"Well that's enough for today; we will see each other again on Thursday. Don't forget that I am available for the next two hours in my office to review your exams if necessary."

As she packed up her things, Theresa glanced at Marie's notes: the offensive sentence from the professor in large block lettering and a list of Emma Bovary's qualities with check marks beside almost all of them.

The young woman admired Kay's face; she could tell that this worn woman was once a beauty; the pictures around the unkempt house were proof of this. The two ladies relaxed now on the porch: the younger sitting on the stairs, Kay in her hand carved antique rocking chair, staring off in contemplation.

"Would you like me to sweep the leaves off your porch?"

"You will learn someday that the beautiful arrangements of leaves that nature places ever so carefully in front of you aren't to create work for you but, rather, to be admired by you." Kay said knowingly as she studied the remaining leaves on the towering maple tree in her yard. She watched as they would fall in turn and calmly dance through the air down to the earth.

"What is it like to get old?" the young girl asked.

"Aside from the fact that it is morbidly depressing, it is actually quite beautiful."

"Was your husband very old when he died?"

Kay didn't answer the girl's question but she did reply, "If you meet someone when you are young, perky and without a lot of flaw, as it goes, then they can always remember you as such. The problem is that, after the usual first divorce, when you get together with someone, you have a body that has lived a little, or a lot. I am guessing this is why the majority of older men sway towards the youth of the opposite sex….. just my guess; they don't enjoy a body that has seen the world. There is a point to this.

If you are with someone at a young age and you marry, possibly have some children and live to reach a nice old age without either of you running away, then there is a *chance for appreciation of the aging process instead of complete and utter fear. You can watch each other deform into what you once had only seen through your grandparents. The loving husband can lift up her saggy breasts and tell her that she's deflated while she glances downwards to state that she is not the only one.*

I suppose there is a reason that love needs to be part of a marriage; everything else will eventually fall away."

The girl recognized that Kay didn't want to answer the question about her husband so she opted to take part in the conversation that her elder seemed to want to have. "Everyone I know is pairing off and taking their short trip down the aisle in a frenzy to avoid loneliness…..or something. I watch people together and wonder how long, or short they will last because there seems to be more hope than love in their relationship. What does it take to happily age with another person?"

"What it comes down to for me, aside from love of course, is loving the changing body of you partner; as long as attraction is there, a lot of things will work themselves out. The next important thing would have to be humor…I often see bitterness in couples who have been together for many years when they forget to laugh."

"Sometimes in couples who aren't even married yet", the girl added.

"If you can play and laugh together through the times, than it is a hell of a lot easier to be happy. I am sure it is different for everyone…seeing as everyone is different. People seem to get so caught up in an idea of what marriage is, or should be, that they don't pay attention to what they have and how wonderful it is. Life is very short in the grand scheme of things; you should be living your life beside someone instead of sitting across from them in a court room." Kay took in a deep breath and stopped rocking in her chair.

She looked at the girl and continued, "Love is a very fickle thing. Everyone feels something like love when they are smitten at the start of a relationship, this fades and then you are left with what? Most of the time, observing the divorce rate, you are left with an ideal that your relationship couldn't live up to. Sometimes though, if you are really lucky, you are left with someone who will worship you until death do you part; someone who will laugh at your jokes and will kiss your wrinkled body because they want to; someone who loves you, despite you.

My husband was not young when he died, but he certainly was too young."

As Marie's cousin, a priest by profession, led the eulogy with some brief biographical words about her life, James studied the room. He had thought that he knew everyone in her life but he recognized only about a quarter of the people there. He sat in the second row behind her immediate family, her mother and father at either end of the pew that was otherwise filled with her brothers.

James was brought back from his thoughts when the priest asked him to come up and say a few words. The mournful attendees simultaneously turned towards him as he rose and made his way up to the front. He smiled to himself when he turned to see that the room was packed full and many were standing at the back; Marie would be pleased; James wondered where she stood watching.

He approached the podium and stood noticing Katherine trying not to weep before he was given a kind nod to begin from the holy man. James took some papers out of his pockets and tried to iron the out with his hand. He looked back at the casket but quickly decided to focus on the crowd instead. He cleared his throat which resonated through the silent room.

He nervously began, "Marie was a woman who never really knew what she wanted but who certainly did know what she didn't want. When she felt something, it was infectious; when she felt nothing, she was intriguing.

She was a person who could be as admired as she was sometimes detested. She was everything from the brightness of the sun to the darkness of the hollows. She laughed at tragedy and cried when humored. She was simultaneously black and white while inspiring every shade of color. She walked a fine line between insanity and clarity, dedication and betrayal, a flake and a genius; she was everything you wish you could be but nothing that she aspired to. She was sadness. She was ecstasy. She was madness. She was" James paused when he lost his place.

He wiped his face with his sleeve and continued on. "We all knew her as we wanted to; no one knew her as she really was. I say these words because I now know them to be true. I fear that I may never know myself without her, that I will never be the man that I was with her in my life. I was warned by many people to run in the other direction when I met her. I was told that she could never love someone and stay happy with them." The crowd of people started to buzz but the noise didn't last long as James was waiting to continue. "I stayed with her despite what people thought they knew about her. She loved me like I have always wanted to be loved and I treasured every second of her affection. Marie, you were the strongest person I have ever met, stronger than you should have been. I hope, more than anything, that you don't hurt anymore. Thank you for sharing your life with me."

There was a still silence among his audience. James looked to Katherine whom had stopped crying for the length of his rambling. He couldn't determine if people thought his words were inappropriate or heartfelt and he didn't much care anymore. He was actually surprised that Marie hadn't written the speech for him before she died. He thanked everyone for listening and made his way back to his seat so that Father Carl could finish up the mourning session.

Someone had a violent cough across the aisle to his left, James looked to see that it was Marie's psychiatrist Dr. Birmingham holding a handkerchief to his mouth. Marie had admired that man, though James never really understood her attachment to an old doctor whom she would talk to every month about nothing much in particular. James had always wondered how Marie had really felt about her mental state because she would never talk about it, in fact, she would never really acknowledge her disorder at all. Personally he felt that her little bit of insanity made her beautiful. He remembered never really knowing what to expect when he got home late at night.

The phone rang. Marie looked away from the computer screen to check who the caller was. The phone continued to ring. Once she started her process of thinking it was difficult for her to stop, with few exceptions. This call was not an exception. She continued to search for more information on the internet about ways and places she could further educate herself. The idea came to her when James suggested that they move somewhere else and that he was thinking about going back to school. And, to observe her mind as it is, she thought to herself:

if i take fashion design he can take carpentry and we could move in with my mother to save money or maybe i'll take photography this school isn't very good what about toronto but can he go there to we could take the train i think he mention something once about architecture but where i need to email my professor i need to check my email i should email someone i haven't emailed in a long time to say hi i haven't seen lisa in a long time i should drop her a line i am shaking a little bit i am hungry i should make a nice big meal for james when he gets home maybe i could take fashion design and photography at the same time if they let me i should apply for summer jobs what books do i need for this summer course i should look it up i have to pee is it wine time i can hold it i am fat i should work out everyday i am going to get all my school work done for the next month i should write a list when am i going to start that painting no time now no time now we should take a vacation together no we can't i should save up secretly to surprise him i need a job this job looks good i should change my resume i should write an awesome resume for james i could surprise him with a good job for him i should wash the dishes before he gets home...

She got up from her seat and went into the kitchen...*the sink is plugged i'll organize these dishes and do them later i want wine no i should call him to see if i can open a bottle i will just have a glass that's okay where's the opener i should write about how crazy my thoughts are there it is i am going to lose this weight by connor's wedding fuck everyone am i repulsive i'll only have a glass it smells nice i think i'll start writing this tastes divine i'll just pick some music start playing solitaire and calm down a bit have i had this before who bought this? i love this song, it reminds me of the first time we slept together. Who ever invented the game of solitaire is a genius.*

A hint of cigar and ripe plum; beautiful. Oh shoot I forgot to email my professor; oh well I can do it later.

The phone rang. Marie looked away from the computer screen to check who the caller was. She picked up the phone and answered, "Hey honey."

"How was your day?" asked James on the other end.

"I got a lot done today."

"Well I am done work." He announced advertising his fatigue.

"Seriously? Already? I just started writing."

"That's okay I have to shower and everything anyway so you can take your time."

"Okay, take your time."

"See you soon."

As she hung up the phone he walked in the door.

"You could have told me how close you were", she said with an equal amount of surprise and irritation.

He smiled as he walked through the apartment, "that would ruin all my fun." James entered their bedroom and kissed her on the back of her head while her eyes stayed fixed on the screen and her fingers didn't stop typing. He recognized that he was intruding at the moment so he walked away towards the kitchen.

"What the hell happened in here?"

Marie yelled from the bedroom, "I organized the dishes, I thought you would be later." She got up and walked towards the kitchen, "I got a lot done today though, so it's not like I was just sitting around. I ordered some pamphlets for information for you to go to school and I printed off some information for you to read. Did you ever tell me you wanted to be an architect or did I make that up? Well we can go to school together and maybe do an exchange overseas together…but we can talk more about that later. Are you hungry?"

"You're speaking very quickly and randomly. Are you feeling a little manic?"

"Yeah. I am"

"What do you want to do tonight then?" he asked as he turned to brew some coffee.

"I don't know, we could play that game you taught me."
"Why don't we watch a movie?"
"Because you'll fall asleep", she said smiling.
"Exactly."
"Come on, you have to stay up with me", she whined pulling on his sleeve like a child.
"Marie, I am human; humans sleep. I know that this is hard for you to understand seeing as you are crazy sometimes but I really need to sleep a little bit tonight. I will stay up as late as I possibly can but then you have to let me sleep. Baby, don't you have any pills left you can take to knock you out?"
"I don't like taking pills for everything. Besides I have been getting a lot done lately."
"I know baby", he said as he kissed her on the forehead, "it's just hard for me sometimes; hard for me to keep up with you."
"You wanna read what I wrote tonight, you're going to love it."
"Sure, I would love to read what you wrote tonight."
"Can you read it out loud again?"
"Of course….there is nothing I would rather do."

James wiped a tear from his eye as a young girl sang Amazing Grace and her brothers arose to perform their pallbearer duties. Not one of them had any sort of expression on their face; James questioned whether that would last or not. What the boys lacked in emotion Katherine more than compensated for, hunched over weeping, her ex-husband slid down the wooden pew to comfort her. *I wonder if the two of them will ever make peace,* James thought to himself doubtingly before he stood up to follow his lover's body out to the hearse.

F reeman took Katherine's arm and said forcefully, "we need to go". She looked at him in sorrow and asked him to go ahead without her; she didn't want to share this moment with him. He shook his head at her with anger and stormed away alone.

June approached her and asked, "Would you like me to wait for you outside?"

She nodded to her friend and took a moment to collect herself before forcing her weak body to rise and continue. As she walked up the aisle behind a pack of young women she felt a gentle touch at her back. As Katherine turned she recognized a comforting face; he embraced her. She didn't cry this time though; she pulled her face from her chest and looked up at Chris' face towering above her.

"I am sorry I didn't call you to tell you", she said feeling guilty.

"I expect that you haven't been thinking straight the last few days."

"How did you find out?" she asked him.

"James called me anticipating that you wouldn't"

"Can you believe this is actually happening?"

"No. No I can't." Chris said with tears in her eyes.

"When did your flight get in?"

"This morning; it is an open ticket so I can stay as long as I need to." Chris said hoping that she would consider his offer.

"I am glad you could make it."

"We can talk more later. Go ahead; they'll be looking for you." He said gently pushing her to the exit.

"I really am sorry I didn't call you", she said.

"I know."

Katherine turned and walked away from Chris, the only man that she had ever loved. He watched her walk away and thought about how much she had changed. She was once the most gorgeous woman in her office, on her street, and in her group of friends. She was so graciously beautiful that it surprised people when she would open her mouth to reveal a strong, sarcastic, and hilarious personality. As she walked away from him on this day, he saw that Katherine was just a shadow of that person, a dark version of her younger self.

He turned towards the space where the casket had rested mere moments before. He approached the stand where people had placed photos of the deceased. He reached his hand out to touch a photo that he had taken of Marie laughing on a trip to visit him. He touched her rosy cheek in the photo and thought of how she resembled her mother at that age. He could remember a time when Katherine had looked just as happy.

Chris came out of the bathroom half shaven, smiling, after making a joke. Katherine was laughing hysterically on the bed, half covered with the white sheet, with a cigarette in hand. He threw down his razor and ran towards the bed hurdling himself on top of her. He kissed her passionately on her lips and she turned away from him. Katherine pushed him off of her, put out her smoke, and reached for her underwear. She became very detached and sad as she dressed.

"We better get going or you'll miss your flight", she said coldly.

"Are you okay?" Chris was confused by the sudden change in mood.

"Of course I'm alright, don't be ridiculous."

"I wish you wouldn't get so sad whenever I leave you", he said lovingly.

"I'm not sad. Nor do I really care if you ever come back." Katherine's back was facing him as she blurted out her hurtful words.

"Why do you say things like that? It's okay for you to miss me you know."

"Hurry up now, we need to get going."

Chris figured out why she was acting so guarded. "Stop acting like I won't be coming back."

"You never know."

"Kate…Please."

"Come on, let's get going", she said as if feeling nothing.

He dressed and packed while she closed up the cottage. There was very little conversation as she drove him to the airport. Katherine was thinking about how to tell him how she felt about him and he was trying to sort out where the day went wrong.

She walked him to the departures and, for the first time, he saw her cry. Until now he believed her unable to shed a tear and, yet, here she was coming undone. He took her into his arms and held her as close to him as he could, not knowing how to make things better for her. She looked up at him unresponsive and he felt a million miles away from her; she was a professional at putting distance between them. Chris was determined to break the silence.

"It's alright" he said.

"Thank you for saying so."

"I will call you next week to make plans. Be good."

He kissed Katherine on the forehead to show his affection for her and then promptly on the lips to show his passion for her. She was salty from her tears. He left feeling uneasy; she left him feeling nauseous.

Chris wept sitting on the pew, the room was now empty and the former occupants were lingering outside the doors. He raised his head to face the collage. He stood and approached the photographs to examine them again. There was one that made him particularly pensive; Marie was days old posed beside a stuffed bear accenting her tiny size. He peeled the photograph from the cardboard background and held it against his chest. Sometimes a memory can hurt more than a fresh wound.

Chris held the phone tightly to his ear and asked, "What do you mean she is on vacation?"

"Sir, I am telling you, Katherine is away for two weeks with her husband", a female voice told him.

"You must be mistaking her for someone else."

"I think I know who I am replacing right now. Would you like to leave a message?"

He hung up the phone and immediately dialed Katherine's mother's house where she had been staying. On the third ring someone picked up.

"Hello?"

"Hi. Is this Mrs. Latendre?" he asked nervously.

"It is, may I ask who is speaking?"

"It's Christopher Stephenson, a friend of your daughter. I tried getting a hold of her at her office but…"

"She is on her honey moon. I think it inappropriate that you are calling here at all."

"Why? I mean I am sorry but who did she marry? How long was she engaged?"

"Well Mr. Stephenson I wasn't informed of the wedding until after it had taken place so I can't really answer your questions. She married a lawyer, I do know that. Will that be all or do you have any more questions I cannot answer?"

"Um, how long was she with this guy, don't you think it's strange that they got married this fast?"

Her mother chuckled and said, "If I know Kate, there is a good reason that they got married this fast and I am sorry but I need to excuse myself from this conversation, have a good day Mr. Stephenson."

Mrs. Latendre hung up before he could sway her to talk some more. Chris placed the phone on the receiver and stood with his hand on the phone for a few moments before it occurred to him. Katherine was pregnant.

Staring at the picture of this beautiful little infant reminded him of those years of uncertainty as if it were yesterday. The pain he felt then was only matched with the tragedy of today. He proceeded to rip more pictures from the collage down and place them gently into his pocket. He had pictures of Marie that her mother had sent him over the years to torment him. These pictures were better though, these pictures were meant to make people feel better about her absence rather than feel bad about her existence.

Lillian and Connor drove towards the cemetery, their hands linked; they each sat silent and pensive. Together they resembled an exotic couple from a faraway land; both olive skinned and dark haired. Both lacked formal education but were hyper intelligent due to the sheer amount of reading they did; anyone who spoke to them were almost instantly intrigued by them.

The truth of it though is that Connor was just the black sheep of his litter and though most people thought Lillian to resemble an exotic goddess from Greece or Iran, she was just a curly haired malado kid from Kalamazoo Michigan.

As they drove, neither was crying, nor had they been. They experienced the world differently than most others. The radio was on low volume but when Neil Diamond's 'Sweet Caroline' came on Lillian turned it up and the two sang off tune at the top of their lungs. As it ended Connor reached to turn the volume down to make a request, "You wanna skip out on the burial and get hosed?"

"Ha! I don't think we should do that today", his wife told him smiling.

"Why not? Marie would if she were us. She would go to some dive pub and toast 'to Connor and Lillian, two hosebags that I loved'."

Lillian laughed at his attempts to convince her, "I don't doubt the truth in that statement but seriously babe, I would really like to go."

"I know….but I had to try; these people are so fuckin depressing"

"Yeah but they're related to you. You know Marie would be with us on this one."

"You know what? I'm pretty sure she would want us to buy a bottle of Shiraz and go sit on a hilltop discussing the finer points in life", he said confidently.

"Maybe, if we mostly discuss how awesome she was. You know she'll be sitting with us judging our conversation and whether or not it was worth skipping her burial."

"I can do that, do you have your book with you?" he asked.

"Let me check" Lillian searched through her purse, "I do."

"This is perfect, we can swing by the liquor store and head over to Fergusson Park to read quotations by her favorite authors and reflect, maybe even fool around a little."

"Your mom is going to be pissed, you know she won't understand.", Lillian said as a last resort to resist the temptation of skipping the burial.

"I don't care do you?" he asked with a smirk.

"Not that much", she admitted.

"Then stop giving excuses that you don't stand by."

"Okay."

Connor pulled to the side of the road and out of the funeral procession. As he and Lillian patiently waited they watched the rest of the cars passing them by. His mother's car had tinted windows but he knew she noticed him there and that she was already mad; she was always mad at him for being different. A baby blue Buick pulled up beside them with the music blasting; Lillian could hear them listening to Pink Floyd. Connor's brothers Jones rolled down the passenger side window and Matt turned down the music.

"What are you guys doin?" asked Jones.

"We're gonna skip right to the drinking, this is not our scene. Come with us, we're heading over to Fergusson Park after the liquor store", Connor explained.

Jones and Matt exchanged looks and Matt said, "Nah, we'll meet you at the park after we bury her. Dude…you're a pallbearer."

"Yeah I know, will you work something out for me?"

Matt laughed awkwardly "Yeah I guess so. People aren't going to think this is cool; missing your sister's funeral is like a major faux pas."

"I don't agree with that do you?" Connor asked with a smile.

Jones thought about it and said, "Nah, not really....I'll meet you at the park after, pick me up some rye okay man?"

Matt yelled out, "I want Jameson's!"

Connor gave a nod, "No problem, see you guys soon. Don't drop the casket!"

Jones and Matt laughed and pulled away; Jones gave the couple the peace sign with his two fingers and then held up his lonely middle finger. Connor turned the car around and drove in the direction of intoxication while Lillian leafed through her notebook of quotes that she had recorded. As she flipped through the book she found a page in Marie's atrocious handwriting. She read it over and smiled.

"Did Marie ever finish that book that she talked about?" Lillian asked.

"I dunno," Connor replied, "she hadn't mentioned it in a long time, why?"

"Nothing I just read something she recorded in my notes, I think it's a quote from Tom Robbins."

"At least she picked a great person to quote, let me hear it."

"Okay...*A book no more contains reality than a clock contains time. A book may measure so-called reality as a clock measures so-called time; a book may create an illusion of reality as a clock creates an illusion of time; a book may be real, just as a clock is real (both more real, perhaps, than those ideas to which they allude); but let's not kid ourselves-- all a clock contains is wheels and springs and all a book contains is sentences.*"

Connor drove, taking in the words while Lillian repeated the passage for proper absorption purposes.

"What book is that from?" he asked.

"I don't know it doesn't say."

"We should find out."

"Okay...there is another one here she wrote out that is also by Monsieur Robbins", she said with a French accent.

"Let's hear it."

"The price of self-destiny is never cheap, and in certain situations it is unthinkable. But to achieve the marvelous, it is precisely the unthinkable that must be thought."

"Exactly!" Connor yelled gloriously.

"Exactly what?" she wondered.

"Some might consider skipping your sister's funeral as unthinkable, but I thought it. In fact, I did it. And damn it, I think that's marvelous!"

"It certainly is babe", Lillian laughed.

"What do you want to drink?" Connor asked as he put the car in park and opened his door.

"I'll drink red wine today to toast the dead."

"Okay, be right back" Connor ran into the liquor store and Lillian remained in the car listening to Nick Drake. She smiled to herself knowingly; he was feeling bad about missing the funeral. She thought to herself and laughed lovingly, *you can take the boy out of the Catholic Church but you can't take the Catholic guilt out of the boy.*

At the burial site James went from hysterics to moments of silent contemplative staring and back again. Chris approached the lost young man and placed a calm hand on his back and offered him a tissue.

"I don't need it" James said with frustration.

"You have snot all over your face...you need it." Chris pushed the tissue into his hand.

"Thank you" he said taking the offering from Chris' hand and wiping his face. "I'm glad you could get here in time."

"Thanks for the call."

"Did you come alone?" James asked him.

"Yes."

The two stood silently before James thought of something to say, "It looks like it might rain doesn't it?"

"I hope it holds out, that would really cut the proceedings short."

"It will rain. Well, it will rain if Marie has anything to do with it."

"She almost always did get her way", Chris said with a smile that gave away his admiration of her constant determination and his inability to say no to her.

James nodded, "It will rain."

The two men looked to their right to see the casket approaching. It was the darkest wood that James had ever seen and he wondered if it was naturally that way or if it had been dyed. There were women trailing behind the casket carrying the flowers that were to be placed on her when she was to be lowered. They were the whitest flowers that he had ever seen; Marie wasn nowhere near as innocent as her mother portrayed her to be. James noticed that Connor was missing and one of Thomas' friends was there in his place. Two of her brothers were trying not to smile as they toted her dead weight past the neighboring gravestones. James wished to himself that he was in on the joke; he knew he would appreciate their brutally inappropriate contentment if he was in on it.

The burial was a grim event to say the least. If it were a movie it couldn't have been arranged to be more depressing. Katherine arranged for a violin to play in the background while each person could drop a cluster of white lilacs on her casket to say goodbye.

Only one person threw themselves on her wooden container and broke down, surprising to most it was her younger brother Thomas. Besides the dramatic explosions there were no dry faces and there were numerous outward bawlers; even the smirking pallbearers had tears to shed when it came down to it. James, through his weeping hic ups, asked Chris, "I have never lost someone so close to me, have you?"

"Yes. I have." He replied with a grim face.

"Is it always this hard?"

"Yes. It is."

As the casket, drowned in wilting spring flowers, was being lowered Chris recalled the last funeral he had attended; his mother's.

He remembered forcing Katherine to let his mother meet Marie before she died. The youth was only twelve at the time but she stood out even then. The last time he spoke to his mother she was in a hospital bed and he was waiting for the inevitable.

"She is yours, I know it", his mother had told him.

"I believe that too, it's just so hard" he admitted as he cried for her fate.

"Kids are hard, no matter how close you are, no matter how hard you try."

Chris lowered his head to hide his tears, "I just don't know what else to do."

"You will, Chris dear, everything happens for a reason. You'll figure it out sooner than you think, everything will just work out", she assured him.

He looking into her eyes and asked, "Can I ask you how you are so sure?"

"Her eyes. No one has those eyes except…"

He cut her off, "I know, I thought you would say that."

"Don't worry dear, just be yourself and good things will happen for you."

"I love you mum."

"I love you too Christopher, very much."

Chris raised his head and came back into reality when he was hit with a drop of cold rain. He looked up towards the clouds and was hit again and again in the face with spring raindrops. Nature proceeded to shower down more violently than it had yet this season. As the small aqua grenades fell to the earth, the crowd of mourners scattered and scurried to their respective cars. Chris smiled as he noticed James and a few of the boys standing around the hole in the ground laughing consciously at a joke that not one of them had verbalized.

Elsewhere on a grassy hill Connor and Lillian were doing a little dance in memory of a girl, and they were laughing and happy. Marie loved to dance in the rain; though normally she danced alone.

"Why don't you tell me something about you? I am always chatting away and I am a little tired today." Kay requested of her company.

"What do you want me to talk about?" the young girl asked.

"Tell me about what you know. I know that when I was your age, what about twenty five, that I had many experiences to share. Mind you these days I barely remember my youth at all so it should prove refreshing to hear about yours."

Kay watched as the young woman sat before her in silence, thinking of a secret to divulge.

"Well, when I was a child, I had what my parents called an emotional problem. I like to think that every little girl has the same problem. I cried. I cried if I hurt myself, if someone called me a name, if I stubbed my toe, if I watched something sad, if someone looked at me strangely, if I wasn't included, if my parents fought, if I lost a game, if I was scared or pretty much at the drop of a hat. I cried a lot. The thing about that is that I honestly felt heartbroken every time I cried....I felt that there was no option left but to cry. I kept this habit from birth until I was about fourteen; at fourteen I fell into a deep depression that lasted a few years and in that time I never really stopped crying. You could ask my mother to this day: how was it living with her during her early teens? Her answer would be emotional. I think the only time I wasn't in tears was when I was asleep, life was unbearable and I barely survived."

"So you have a positive view of your childhood. Did things change when you matured?"

"Not exactly, I self medicated with narcotics and as wrong as that is, in the end it served a purpose. After a few years or so of this so called medication I had to go through the great effort of releasing myself from the habit. More crying, more pain.

But alas, in came a ray of sunshine. For about three years after this messy time I was, in a way, completely void of emotion. I don't know if the previous drugs were to blame or whether it was some sort of psychosis, but I walked the earth for years and felt nothing. I felt no pain, nor was I ever very happy; I, for the very first time in my life, did not shed a tear for a long time. It was almost as if I had dried up and had nothing left. I mean, sure, bad things happened but I certainly didn't get upset about them nor did I have any emotional breakdowns like I always had. It was a different part of my emotional life. The part where there were none.

The place where I am now is confusing at best but remains what I believe to be the closest to "normal" that I have ever been. I don't cry all the time nor am I void of emotion. It is funny to me when I think about how long after a telephone commercial that I will cry, but I like that; I like empathy. I no longer obsess over my own state of emotions but can see others and feel what they feel. I suppose it is a loss of self loathing and a positive gain of understanding....I like that. Maybe pills aren't so bad, only time will tell; it is the only way to know anything."

"You tell your story as if you were an elk describing its life by how many times it escaped the hunt. The elk's tale would sooner be admired if it explained how it saw the sunlight break through the canopy of the forest to reveal the beauty of a single flower. He might describe the sensation of grazing through a meadow after a rainfall when all is silent and still."

"Do you find comfort in criticism?" the girl asked.

"As much as you do in self pity", quipped Kay

"Why did you ask me to talk if you were going to be mean about it?"

"It helps me think", Kay replied, "It makes me realize how far I've come."

Michael turned the volume down on the television when he heard Jane's heels step across the hardwood floor above him. He took a breath in to yell to her but thought he might be better off to just make his way upstairs. When he reached the top step she was there, leaning over the kitchen sink, staring deeply into the seemingly hypnotic drain. She raised her head to face the window overlooking their porch; she smiled to hide her frown. Michael, a tall dark and handsome type, was his ever charming self and took her hand to pull her into him, her head resting on his chest and his arms devouring her petite figure.

"Was it terrible?" he asked.

"It was a funeral. It was okay. Her family is weird."

"I should have gone with you", he said with very little sincerity.

"No, I excused you for a reason, don't worry about it."

"How does a glass of wine sound?" Mike offered, craving a drink himself.

"Not as good as vodka water." She left his embrace and walked back to their bedroom to change. She kicked her shoes off at the hall closet. In her bedroom she fell backwards onto the oversized bed and zoned out looking at the ceiling fan above her head. Mike broke her trance when he came in with the clear drink in his hand, it was a triple. He sat on the bed beside her; she didn't move. The drink was then gently placed in her limp hand; the bed did most of the holding.

After a lengthy silence, Jane held her upper body up to take a sip of her drink; she drank half of the glass and dropped her head before she spoke, "I don't think she's dead."

"Yes you do", Mike replied.

"I know. But I don't want to think she's dead." Jane remained horizontal this time and brought the glass to her face, lifting her head ever so slightly. When lazily attempting to sip from the glass, the liquid trickled down her cheeks and down her neck. She lay back down as Mike took off his sock and wiped her skin with it.

"Did you get any answers today?" he asked.

"Not really, there were quite a few theories out there but none that I am a fan of…there is the classic depression theory; this is disproved though because we know she was taking her medication so depression doesn't really fit. The depression thing could work though in another way because the medication deals with brain chemicals I think, so maybe she was depressed because of her life. I know she was pretty stressed. Anyways, another idea that I heard was that it was some freak accident or, better yet that she was murdered…that's my personal favorite."

"Well that is something else", he said laughing.

"Yeah. People are fucked up."

Mike tucked a loose piece of hair behind Jane's ear, "You look pretty tired"

"I had a pretty exhausting day. I think I might skip dinner and try to get some sleep", she said before finishing off her drink and handing him back the glass.

"Okay. Just so you know, Sean is coming over."

"Why?" She asked with anger as she sat up. "We couldn't have a break today?"

"Jane, he was coming over for you. Just because your heart is made of ice doesn't mean other people can't feel bad."

"Whatever. Don't be loud." Jane rolled over so Mike was facing her back. He took her empty glass and left the room, shutting the door behind him. She lay there, exhausted, but her eyes remained open, fixated intensely on the wall.

Jane and Marie had always been a reflection of each other. They would both smile to please people but always held certain sadness behind their eyes. Jane had been the deceased's closest girlfriend though they rarely exchanged personal grievances despite the fact that they carried many. Their friendship started when they split an ecstasy pill in their teens and talked all night discovering how much they had in common. They developed through the years to become each other's greatest pillar of strength.

Jane thought about what she had lost this week and how surreal it was watching Marie's body being lowered into the ground.

She listened to Mike make dinner, load the dishwasher, and flip through the television stations. She heard Sean arrive and make inappropriate comments about the deceased. She was not angry; she wasn't much of anything at that moment but tired. She remembered her friend, talking, crying, and laughing. She remembered how she looked and the way she would speak. They had never fought. They had never raised their voices to each other nor had they very often even differed in opinion.

Jane longed to fight with her now.

Charles pulled into his driveway and turned the key in the ignition of his Mercedes. He coughed into a handkerchief and popped a cough drop in mouth. He sat for a moment watching his wife's figure through the kitchen window; she was a shadow to him but he recognized her movement.

He sat waiting for some force to coach him out of his car and into his house but it didn't come. While he waited he thought of his patient. He wondered how he could be so wrong about someone's mental state; how he didn't see any signs. He wondered why she would lie to him.

He noticed his wife look out at him through the front window so he got out of the car and made his way to the front door where he took the mail from the mailbox. Cynthia always entered through the garage and would forget to pick up the letters and bills. He unlocked the front door and, as he entered, flipped through the envelopes. He still, after forty years, enjoyed seeing Dr. Birmingham written on paper. It was one of his only remaining pleasures. This personal pride was interrupted by his wife. "So….?"

"So what?" he asked, hoping this wouldn't turn into a fight.

"How was it?"

"It was quick, the rain cut it short."

"Did anyone seem upset with you?" she asked him.

He noticed that she was slurring her words. He took his coat off and hung it over the kitchen chair. "Why do you do this to me?"

"Because you are a fraction of a man; because you are a bad psychiatrist; because you keep killing people."

"You know that's not true."

"Do I?" she asked sarcastically.

"It is just chance that I have been the doctor for a run of suicidal people lately."

"They probably kill themselves when they realize that the person supposed to help them is more pathetic than they are." Cynthia spurted out at him, stabbing her husbands ego.

Charles took the almost empty bottle of wine and poured himself a glass. He brought the glass to his face and breathed in the aroma as he took some of the wine into his mouth. He swallowed and began, "Jim was my patient for all of a day when he jumped in front of a train. He was beyond my help at that point, or beyond any help I could give him in twenty-four hours. Amy hadn't been to see me in over a year, I had no idea how poorly she was doing until I received the call saying that she had shot herself. Amy's mother was never really my patient; we just spoke about her daughter. I really wasn't assessing her and even if I had I doubt I could have guessed that she would slit her wrists two weeks after her daughter's death."

"What about this one?" she asked with spite.

He took the wine glass to his nose again but, this time, poured all that was left in the glass down his throat. The liquor soothed his throat. Charles jogged down to the wine cellar to choose another bottle, he decided on a vintage from the year Marie was born. He slowly climbed back up the stairs knowingly avoiding the demon in the kitchen for a few moments. He came back in the cold room to see that Cynthia had not moved from where he left her.

"I asked you a question."

"Yes, you did. What was that again?" he said mocking her.

"What is your excuse for this one?" she repeated.

"No excuse."

"So why did she kill herself?"

"I DON'T KNOW." Charles yelled. He collected himself and repeated, "I don't know."

"How convenient", she hissed.

Cynthia filled her glass and walked out of the room, Charles heard her stumble on the stairs and hoped that she would go to bed for the night. Charles escaped to the living room after opening his bottle and turned the television on; he watched the news but thought about Marie. *Why would she kill herself,* he wondered. *She was the most self aware person I had ever known and she was mentally sound. She had visited me every month for eight years and had turned from a mentally anguished suicidal teen into a model for therapy and treatment. Have I completely missed something? Was she so good at deception that she fooled the one person who was hired to see through such facades? I think I might actually be cursed. Why is my wife such a bitch? Like I haven't done enough for her, stupid cunt.*

Despite his racing mind, Charles faded off to sleep. What seemed like seconds later, he woke to his son shaking his arm. "Dad, wake up. You need to go to bed."

"Jake? Oh, I am going to stay down here I think."

"Okay, sorry I woke you. And mom told me about your patient, sorry about that too."

"Thanks kid. Did your mother also tell you that it was my fault?"

"No offense dad but I doubt that a girl who met with you less than a dozen times a year was effected so drastically by something you said or didn't say that she felt compelled to end her life. In fact, it would be pretty egocentric of you to think so. You were just some guy that she told her problems to, that's it." And that was it; Jake kissed his dad on the forehead and took off upstairs.

Charles smiled to himself and rested his head back on the pillow. The brutal honesty of his son was enlightening and, more importantly, proved his innocence, helping him sleep that night and many more.

As Freeman drove home alone he had much opportunity to think about the closing day. When he got stuck in traffic behind a turned tractor trailer he was trapped with his thoughts. He had felt very unwelcome at his own daughter's funeral; he actually surprised himself when he showed up. Funny how people can be so negative, he thought. He turned his wipers down because the rain was calming. Horns were sounding and he watched as an angry middle aged man stuck his head out his window to yell at the emergency response team. *Funny how people can be so negative*, he thought to himself.

He had attended the funeral to compensate for missing Connor's wedding the year before. He wanted to avoid the negative people; he knew they would castrate him. Negative people, he thought, would never give him a break. Freeman felt that almost everyone was out to get him. He felt this, for the most part, because it was true.

He believed that life dealt him a bad hand; everything was luck, except when he won at the races, that was skill. It was bad luck when he got caught stealing money from his clients. It was worse luck that sent him to jail, but good luck that got him out years early. It was some sort of luck that forced him to abandon all his children but very good luck that ensured one or two still spoke to him, well, one now.

Freeman was a man of great aptitude and, once, great achievement.

THE ART OF DYING

Many once believed that he would be the next Prime Minister; many now claim that he is a schizophrenic. Many years ago he had the world in his hands and he smoothly slipped it into his pocket; he had been driven by greed.

Despite all of his misconduct throughout her life, Marie allowed him to be a part of hers. She spent years debating why but, in the end, realized that if he didn't have her, he would have no one. She felt such empathy for him, mostly because she knew how sad he was and how everyone could see through him now. He didn't even have his lies to comfort him now; not even he could believe his bullshit.

Freeman had no conscious knowledge of these truths but was starting to gather that the world might not be as negative as he thought. He thought of his daughter.

No tears, no guilt, nothing. His mind was making him tired. He reached over and turned on the radio. He put on the baseball game and listened contently to the plays with the comforting background noise of angry car horns and cursing.

T he two women sat on the porch together and the girl felt like talking. "I wrote a poem once. It was actually the first one I ever wrote. It was simple, it rhymed, it wasn't very good, or maybe it was for an eight year old. It was a sad poem. It was a poignant poem about my life, or rather, the lives of those around me."

She paused to see if Kay was interested in this topic at all but there was no reply from her elder so she continued. "I think it talked about a missing father with a business card, walking around not caring that his absence was hard. It might have mentioned a mother yelling down the hall or maybe bumping into some walls. I am pretty sure it recalled a little brother in his bed quiet while his sister curled up crying. I can't really say for sure. I was very proud of it though. When I was nine I decided to start my first novel, it was going to be a fantasy. I was in a dungeon and trying to make my way through it to freedom but every door revealed a new challenge. In retrospect I now know that I was writing out the adventures of my older brothers playing D & D. I thought I was being pretty original but alas, as most writers realize about themselves, I was not. I was doing what my third year professor described as 'writing what you know'. I suppose that is safe. Now I think I write what I know with a twist of what is interesting. Maybe not; I often misjudge what people like."

She stopped to drink some lemonade that Kay had made for her. There was still no complaint from her so the girl kept talking. "I had actually forgotten about this poem until recently when an editor asked me what the first thing I ever wrote that mattered was. I thought about it for less a while when the poem came to mind. I read my words *over and over again because it was the first time that I openly admitted the sadness in my life; it was my secret confession. I had finally been brave enough to take action and express my discontent with the people in my life. Mind you, I did hide the poem so that my mother could never find it. I feared confronting her for she was a woman to fear; today she is a woman to pity, but she does that enough herself.*

These days I do a lot more thinking than actual action. I always wonder if I could have saved her life had I battled her more. Are my failures catching up with me? This is just a time for reflection; action will surely follow. Too little too late perhaps, but better than never."

The woman paused and waited for Kay to speak. The elderly lady stared off down the road at the children playing; it wasn't clear if she had listened to one word from her mouth. Kay reached down to adjust her knee high taupe stockings and when she replaced her skirt over her leg she looked at the young lady whimsically and asked, "What is D & D?"

The younger of the two stared at her knees while shaking her head with disappointment; she then raised her eyes to fix back on Kay and laughed out loud. She spent the rest of their day together explaining the intricacies of the wonderful world of Dungeons and Dragons. Kay was captivated by this game of fantasy. The girl realized why this old woman never seemed interested in what she had to say; the two of them shared the same looming detachment from reality and intrigue in the fantastic.

This was the beginning of a fascinating career inspired, of course, by the one person who wouldn't give her the attention she wanted when she was being honest.

James lay still on the couch where he had lost consciousness the night before; his heart at ease for less than a moment before her laugh resonated in his mind. His eyes opened, focused on the white ceiling, and began to leak. He sat up, shook his head and wiped the tears from his cheek.

He picked up the empty beer bottles and the full ashtray to take them into the kitchen because, despite his state, the mess still bothered him. He opted not to eat, but that a smoke would do. He returned to the couch in order to light up and he could hear her say to him, "is it really necessary to have one right now?" He thought to himself that it was and so, he opened the match box, took three matches out and struck them, causing a large sort of small flame.

With the cigarette in his right hand he placed his palms to his forehead and cried. She had always told him that he wasn't just killing himself with his smoking habit but her as well. He put out his smoke and rested his head on the pillow he had recently abandoned. He could smell her lingering scent on the upholstery and he took it in; his breaths were short and infrequent because he didn't want the aroma to fade too quickly.

He thought of how she would simultaneously laugh and cry while explaining to him that it was all very normal. How she would scream at him and then apologize within seconds; hate him and love him more than anyone had before. How she would cry; but never know why. She was an emotional wreck half the time and then dead inside for the rest. He felt closer to her now, mimicking her emotions.

He fell asleep again, this time dreaming of Marie walking into the apartment as if no time had passed, kissing his cheek where the tears fell and asking what was wrong. This delusion was comforting enough to let him rest for a short while.

He awoke. It seemed the traffic outside his window was especially impatient today. He rolled over and picked up his cell phone to check the time. 12:22. He held the phone in front of him knowing it was going to ring; it rang, and his stomach dropped. Reality sobered him again when he recognized Katherine's number as the caller. He believed this to be a bad way to start his day but, regardless, he answered.

Katherine hung up the phone and stood in her kitchen disheveled and confused. She opened the fridge, searched for the orange juice and settled for the Bailey's. She opened the bottle and filled a mug halfway; when she couldn't muster up the energy to make coffee to finish the drink she settled with ice. She, with mug in hand, staggered to the bathroom and sat on the side of the bathtub. She gazed into her mug of creamy liqueur and decided now was the right time to take a drink; she drank it down like an Irish rugby team having a chugging contest. Since the mug was empty she set it on the rim of the bathtub and readied herself to rise. Her hand slipped and hit the mug which crashed into the tub and smashed into a hundred equally destroyed pieces.

"Shit" she mumbled to herself. "God damn it" she blurted when she heard Tomas coming towards her from his room.

"What the hell did you do now?" he asked when he came around the corner.

"Nothing....a mug fell I think." Katherine muttered looking at the ground.

"You think?" he asked with much anger.

"Ah fuck off" she said bitterly.

Tomas' heart broke as he observed the shape she was in; he wondered if she even remembered that her daughter has died; or maybe the point was to forget.

Tomas was a tall, wiry version of Marie. Everyone always told them that they looked like twins though neither of them agreed. He always ate garbage and Marie always nagged him about it, like a mother should. Despite his awful eating habits, Tomas never gained a pound, a reflection of his luck in life as a whole. Between him and his sister, she seemed to have all of the problems that he should have had; enough poor health to be divided between five people.

He started to clean up the shards and Katherine fiddled with her face in the mirror. She looked at her haggard face; her skin had aged and wrinkled but it was her eyes that gave her away. She looked back at her handsome young son, bent over her mess, struggling to find the tiny fragments that were hiding from him.

"Just leave it." She said frustrated that he was taking so long.

"I would but you would probably hurt yourself later if I didn't clean it now", he replied.

"I am not a child you know."

"I know, children don't drink mass quantities of alcohol."

"You think you're funny don't you smartass?"

Tomas chuckled sadly, "Mom, my sense of humor is the only reason I can live here."

"You couldn't leave me. You wouldn't know how to take care of yourself", she said with a slur.

"Whatever you say mom" he said bitterly under his breath as he dumped the remaining glass into the garbage before he returned to his room.

Katherine held her hand to her head as if she could make the pain go away by doing so; it didn't fade but a slight nausea did present itself. It occurred to her that the caffeine from a coke might help so she made her way into the kitchen and poured herself a half glass of the soda, and mixed it with a half glass of rum. Tomas could hear the ice clinking in her glass and the sound of her bumping into the walls as she climbed the stairs, he was fairly certain that he knew where she was going.

When she reached the summit of the staircase she stood before the innocent white door of her only daughter. She had closed it in denial the evening prior and now was feeling a twinge of guilt for doing so. Instead of entering, as she had planned to do on her way up, she sat on the top step staring at the outside of the door.

Marie's old house coat hung there, waiting patiently for her to return and to take comfort in such an old and worn garment. Katherine had told her so many times to throw the thing away but she wouldn't; Marie loved some inanimate objects more than she did people. Katherine bottoms upped her glass, stood up and gently placed her hand on the faded blue housecoat. There was no true comprehension of the events passed for her, not yet, she had made sure of that by keeping a consistent state of false consciousness. She removed her hand from the tattered clothing and walked away from this door; she knew not at that time but she was not going to pass by that door again for a month, confrontation with Marie was a thing of the past.

Tomas opened the fridge in the kitchen to find nourishment as he yelled to his mother, "are you going to make us something for lunch?" Katherine didn't respond and he assumed that she had passed out again. He sorted through the bags of rotten vegetables and old moldy dinner leftovers and he found nothing edible. The sad thing was that this was always what the fridge looked like. He felt a wave of nausea; his sister used to make food for him when their mother couldn't, and she would have been the one to clean the glass out of the bath tub.

He was distraught; he was alone now. He shook the panicked sadness out of himself, grabbed the car keys, and headed to MacDonald's where he would find solace.

Laying still and quietly in the guestroom, Samson could hear his parents stirring. He knew they would be surprised to see him and impressed that he remembered where the spare key was kept. He could hear the two seniors whispering about the closed door and he debated putting them at ease by revealing his presence; he opted not to. Finally a soft knock at the door and his step mother popped her head inside with a whispered "hello?"

"Hey Judy, it's just me", he said to reassure her.

His step mother yelled down the stairs, "it's just Samson sweetheart, put on the coffee!" She turned back to Samson in his old bed, "You had us wondering there for a minute…we were standing outside your door trying to figure out who might come here unannounced."

Samson, taking the hint, didn't want to reveal his reasoning for the visit so he said nothing but, "well, it's just me."

"Okay then, we'll see you downstairs in a few minutes."

Judy shut the door carefully behind her and descended the stairs; whispering ensued in the kitchen. Samson knew that his mysterious presence was slowing killing the lady of the house, so he smiled and hopped out of bed with little intention of telling her a thing.

He stopped at the mirror and noticed the difference in his own face.

The sadness was there and he wasn't going to be able to hide it from his father. He hopped in the shower with the hopes of washing that look away.

Samson was an average statured, average looking, handsomely feminine man. His smile was irresistible to anyone who knew him but average to others. His hair was half as red as a hooker's lipstick and not much more innocent. Admittedly, especially by Marie, it was the beautiful eyes he carried that defined him. He had gorgeous green eyes with one large fleck of brown in his left eye. Marie always joked that he was so full of shit that it was starting to surface in his features, but he never doubted her admiration for the shit. He had always loved that she made fun of his eye because it meant that she loved it, or at least that she noticed it.

He thought of her as he readied himself for the firing squad downstairs. He descended to the kitchen and noticed Judy out in the garden as his father handed him a large green mug full of strong black coffee. Samson took the mug to his mouth and chuckled, "how much whiskey did you put in my morning coffee?"

"Well, enough to ease your mind first thing in the morning."

"I didn't know my mind needed easing."

"Well, a father knows these things."

"Really?" Samson questioned suspiciously.

"I base my presumption on two factors: you haven't slept in your old room for over ten years and your mother called me yesterday to tell me that you were headed to Marie's funeral."

"I see." Samson felt a twinge of anger thinking of his parents discussing his life over a casual phone call.

"Sorry to hear about Marie, she was a good girl, Judy always loved talking to her."

"She had her moments", Samson replied in an attempt to seem unaffected.

Judy came back in through the sliding doors with white cuttings from her lilac bush mixed with some red tulips. Samson remembered Marie struggling to open the door, a little drunk and not realizing the lock needed to be opened. He stood behind her watching her fight with it; she figured it out eventually and the two laughed at her ignorance.

"Son...what are you dreaming about?" his father asked.

"Nothing much, what were you saying?"

"We are heading out to pick up some mulch for the garden. You want to come along?"

"I think I'll stay here a while if you don't mind."

"I will bring something home for dinner then if you are staying", Judy said while looking at her husband.

"Sounds great, I would appreciate it if you could grab me a toothbrush while you are out."

"Your father will do that for you."

As the couple puttered around the house readying themselves for a much anticipated day of mulch purchasing, Samson slipped out the patio door and found himself on the back porch in the perfectly maintained garden. He stood like a totem, still and stiff, staring at the two wooden chairs placed quixotically side by side. He could see her there, staring up at him, growing frustrated that he would not sit. The difference is that it was almost night when she sat there; she couldn't help but repeatedly say how beautiful the garden was.

Samson sat down in the closest chair to the door. He leaned back and felt the cold hard wood press against his back, a comforting discomfort he thought to himself. He set his coffee down on the arm rest, closed his eyes and remembered.

The air was thick, the day had been hot and the night welcomed rain. The cards were now scattered despondently on the table, the time had passed for innocent games. There was music playing in the house and Marie faintly recognized the soothing voice of Neil Diamond singing love songs for no one. The wine had dwindled to a few ounces that remained in the glasses but neither cared. The sprinklers turned on and devoured Neil, but the silence between them was much more prominent at the time. Samson was uncomfortable in the chair but said nothing still. He wondered why she had come there to be with him; he could only assume that she needed to get away. He wasn't going to ask, nor did he much care.

Samson glanced at Marie's hand; it rested casually on her armrest, unkempt, and boyish. She wore a Band-Aid on her index finger, she had gained a sliver from the chair on which she sat, but she didn't seem to hold a grudge. He placed his right on her left, and their hands embraced. Her face turned towards his and she smiled; he recognized the gratitude and smiled back at her.

    A drop of rain fell from the sky to land on Samson's cheek; he wiped the intruder away with his free hand. They sat and waited while the trespasser's friends came to the party; soon it was showering. Samson began to rise and Marie held his hand tighter to say that she wasn't ready to leave. The two sat and practically drowned in the rain until, much to his surprise, she stood calmly and looked at him through the falling rain drops and said "I am ready to go now."

D*espite the constant crashing of the rain on her roof, Kay heard her front door open and close followed by footsteps that lead into the living room. She was expecting the girl to show up today so she slowly made her way into the small front room with confidence that she had arrived. Hunched on her couch she discovered a sorry version of the confident young lady she was accustomed to. Kay noticed that the soaked girl had curly hair and wasn't as pretty with smudged makeup. Kay took a crocheted blanket from the side of the couch and placed it over the wet shoulders. "To what do I owe the dramatic entrance?" she asked.

The sopping mess lifted her head to look into Kay's eyes; the wise woman knew then not to push her today. The girl was breathing erratically, due to crying and running it would seem. Kay wondered if the dampness would stain her couch; the younger wondered when she should begin and if Kay would be insulted for her grief.

"I hurt myself today. I was caught in a lie, and I destroyed someone that I love. More pertinent though is the fact that I have demolished myself in the backfire. I don't know now whether or not I ever even loved him or if I just loved the lie that we were living. I mean, the whole time we were together I didn't think I cared too much but now, my God. Now that he has hurt me I think about the way he used to smile at me, I think about the way he used to trust me. He was the sweetest thing, and I loved his every fault, even when I was trying to hate him. I let him believe that I was as perfect as he saw me, the lie was that I was just another girl; for a while he looked at me in a way that I will never get back. I am ill, I can't seem to let things be right.

I am deceitful, untrustworthy and immoral. He told me so, and he is not the type to say things like that unless they are true. It hurts Kay, it really hurts, I don't know whether to throw up or step in front of a car."

Kay took the girl into her frail arms and squeezed as tight as she could; the receiver felt the effort and wept in her arms. Kay accidently let a tear fall down her wrinkled cheek. She tried to think of something to say that wouldn't sound too preachy. She decided on, "Self destruction hurts everyone in the vicinity."

Kay paused, thinking that this was sufficient enough for the moment. She let go of the girl who had now calmed. It made her sad to see someone so young in self induced anguish; they had too much in common. She thought of something to add, "Sadness doesn't always have to end in devastation; at times, you can just let it pass uneventfully. Depression doesn't have to finish you."

Taking the blanket off her shoulders, the girl knew that she had come to the right place.

"I know Kay, it's just that sometimes the hurt is the only thing that reminds me how to feel."

Kay silently sat before her and said, "You sound like you should write country songs."

Kay admired her as she smiled, got up off the couch and walked out the door without saying a word.

There was something about that girl, she thought to herself.

A clamoring crash in the kitchen startled Josie as she was changing Amelie's diaper. She picked her plump daughter up and went down the stairs to investigate Matthew's progress with dinner. When she turned the corner she saw her anxious husband amongst complete chaos.

"What happened?" she asked him.

"I don't know, I must still be hung over from last night. Nothing is working for me today."

Josie approached him and stroked his back lovingly. Amelie, his beautiful dark haired princess, put her hands out to her father to be held and he complied.

"You are a successful chef, I have seen you put out hundreds of plates without blinking. I don't think your trouble today is because you are hung over. It is okay to be nervous; you haven't all sat down together in over ten years."

"Here, take her, I need to get back to it", Matthew handed his daughter back to Josie.

"They will be arriving soon, do you want my help?"

"No, I just need some time…was that the door?"

"I think so, don't worry, I'll get it", she said absorbing some of his nervous energy.

As she walked towards the door with Amelie in hand it occurred to Josie that she was going to be face to face for the first time with Matthew's father: a disturbing vindictive creature that, until now, has been nothing more than a scary bedtime story.

To her pleasant surprise as she opened the door, the caller was Jones, a 6f5 god of war, or so he looked. His hair mimicked Madusa's with his dancing long black dreads, highlighted with well-deserved grey hairs winding through the intricate knots. Those dark eyes of his told a story that everyone appreciated yet no one understood. His smile was like all of the siblings; it lit up the room and forced others to imitate the gesture.

Josie, who stood a foot below him, welcomed him in and took the bottle of Jameson's from his hand and thanked him. Jones admired Matthew's matching wife and daughter, he leaned over to pinch Amelie's cheek and kiss her on the forehead before he inquired about the whereabouts of his younger brother. She promptly directed him to the kitchen and, though she wanted to, she didn't warn him of Matthew's disposition. As Jones headed down the corridor she noticed her daughter fading and so she took her up to put her down for a nap. Downstairs, Jones questioned his brother's intentions, "Are you nervous?"

"No." was the reply.

"Do you know when he should get here?"

"Soon", Matthew said vaguely.

"Do you know why you invited him over?"

"I am starting to wonder why I invited you." The younger brother replied honestly.

"Just curious what you think is going to happen today." The elder said protectively.

"I just thought it would be nice if he had a chance to reconnect with us. He hasn't even seen Amelie before, he might not even know she exists."

"I'm sure Marie would have mentioned it to him", Jones assured him.

"Yeah, that's true" Matthew said as the doorbell rang, "can you get the door?"

Jones nervously walked down the hall not wanting to be the first to confront the man often referred to among them as 'the devil'. To prepare himself he yelled out "who is it", and then, relieved, opened the door to Connor, Tomas and Lillian. He noticed that the latter two had been crying, likely, he thought, it was Marie's fault. He thought they made an amusing threesome as fair haired Tomas awkwardly towered over the other two, both of whom had dark wiry hair and Persian skin. After the usual greetings and fun poking, Connor asked Jones, "What is this all about?"

"I don't know, Matt's living in a dream world. He is hoping that the devil is going to walk through his door, hug and kiss him, and they will skip off into the sunset singing show tunes and living happily ever after."

"Does he remember my wedding? I am surprised that guy even showed up at Marie's funeral." Connor said abruptly.

"I know, let's indulge him though, he is really stressed right now."

"Where is Matty?" asked Connor.

"Where do you think?" Jones said nodding his head in the direction of the kitchen.

The pack roamed into the kitchen and Connor immediately started helping Matthew with the food; the two had worked together professionally for years and it was obvious. Lillian opened the magnum of Malbec that they brought and listened to her new family nervously discuss everything but what was on their minds the most. Tomas stood there watching his brothers, feeling angry that they didn't seem bothered by the fact that their sister died days before. Josie joined the group and welcomed the new comers. She noticed the patriarch had not yet arrived and so she asked, "what time are we expecting Freeman?" The room fell silent before Tomas asserted, "He's not going to come."

"He will come" Matthew said impatiently.

"People change Tommy, don't be so negative," Lillian blurted for Matt's benefit, noticing she was due for a refill.

"Dinner is going to be ready soon though, I hope he isn't too much longer or we might have to start without him" Matthew added as he tossed a small salad in an oversized wooden bowl. "Jones, go throw a cd in would you."

"No problem bro."

Jones entered the living room with the intention of putting on some sort of uplifting music to soothe the hearts of his kin but, after assessing his choices he played something to honor the woman lost. Jones played a

Dead Can Dance album, one of Marie's favorites. He opted to highlight her absence rather than ignore it, this choice of the eldest made the youngest and Lillian rather pleased. Tomas had never heard the album but when Lillian thanked Jones for his choice and explained Marie's love for this music, Tomas proved to be a little more at ease.

When the phone rang everyone froze; they assumed the obvious and Matthew ran to the phone, knowing very well who was calling at this time. "Hello?" he said nervously, "Hi, we were just wondering what was holding you up"; he spoke as his family stood listening intently. "Well, dinner is ready but we can wait if you think you are going to be late." "Um, yeah, I guess, but…" he paused and his company held their breath. "We can wait for you, this dinner is for you…" Jones and Connor exchanged knowing looks while Lillian placed her hand supportively on Tomas' hand. "Well, if there is no way then I guess we will just eat without you." He continued with his hand on his forehead, "No, I understand, don't worry about it… yeah….you too…have a good night."

Matthew looked at the portable phone and hung up. He looked up at his brothers and they knew that Freeman had cancelled. "He got held up at work and his van is in bad shape." Matt set the phone down not so gently and exerted "At least we still have a great meal to eat." He then stormed out of the room and up the stairs with Josie trailing behind him.

Jones and Connor looked to Tomas and shook their heads simultaneously. Lillian asked, "who wants more wine", and the three remaining men answered in agreement "me".

Dinner, when it was served, proved to be depressing with a hint of self pity. There were few words and less interjection. Tomas, the youngest, came forth with the most mature question proposed this evening. "Are we sad now because a man who has always disappointed us and abandoned us when we needed him most has successfully done it to us again or are we sad because a girl who we have all secretly spited has killed herself and proven her undying worth to us?"

Jones answered, "I think we are silent because both people have betrayed us in ways that we can't easily accept. "

Lillian added, "I don't actually care about a man who has done nothing but hurt the people I love, but I do miss one of my closest friends who has chosen, for whatever reason, to leave this earth. And, for the record, we don't know that she killed herself"

Tomas nodded and added "I second that notion."

Connor concluded, "Well we are all feeling a variety of emotions right now, that doesn't mean that we can't enjoy dinner."

Matthew couldn't help but ask, "Why wouldn't he just come, what did he have to lose?" Josie pat him lovingly on the back.

Tomas raised his body up and threw his fist down onto the table, "!HE DOESN"T CARE ABOUT US, HE NEVER HAS, HE NEVER WILL. HE DOESN'T CARE ABOUT THIS DINNER, HE DOESN'T CARE ABOUT ANYONE BUT HIMSELF!"

Matthew looked up at Tomas and calmly asked him to leave. Connor attempted to explain the younger's reaction but was also asked to evacuate the premises by his brother. So the two men left with Lillian and didn't fight their brother's request because they knew that he had something secretly invested in this evening's dinner, though they knew not what. They politely said goodbye so that Matthew would know that he was already forgiven for kicking them out; he told them he would call them tomorrow so that they would know he was sorry for his actions. And so they were gone and Matthew was left with a fully set dinner table and only Jones and Josie to enjoy it with him; he knew that he had to answer to them, and he was dreading when the questions would start.

Josie left the table to check on Amelie upstairs in case she was woken by the yelling. Jones turned to Matthew with the smile that never really left his face in any situation and he asked, "what did you want to happen tonight?"

"Nothing", was the frustrated response.

Jones thought something out long and hard before he said it. "You have always disliked her and you have done a terrible job of hiding it. Since she was born you have rejected her, which is strange because she was born only a few years after you; I thought you would have made good friends."

"Friends", Matthew repeated the word with disgust.

Jones continued, "I am going to tell you what I think. I think you hated how much attention she got over the years because she was sick. I think, when you wanted love and affection from your parents, you didn't get it because she was sucking them dry with her issues. When you would get your straight A's in high school, she was getting kicked out of school because of her breakdowns. I also think that you held that against her when you should have held it against them."

"It's not that." Matthew sat contemplating whether or not he would talk this out with his brother. He decided that he would rather him know the truth than think the reason was because of petty jealousy. "It is something bigger."

"That's okay, tell me about it."

"Do you remember when mom and dad broke up the first time?"

"Sure do. What were you, like two?" Jones asked trying to remember the year.

"No, I was four. I had an earache and I wouldn't stop crying and there was nothing mom could do to make the pain go away. I remember dad came into my room and told her to leave me alone for a while and to stop coddling me. They started to fight about it and that night he left the house."

Jones nodded, "I remember that too, I could hear them fighting from my bedroom because it was right next to yours".

Matthew continued, "Well dad didn't come back after that and a few months later mom told us she was pregnant again. Dad still didn't come back until Marie was born. I remember hearing him say that nothing could keep him away from his little princess. You see? I was the reason their marriage ended and she brought the family back together."

"Matt, that's crazy. Their marriage ended because dad was a selfish prick and mom was a raging alcoholic. Don't put that shit on yourself. And Tomas was born right after Marie, why don`t you hate him?"

"Because Marie spent her whole life trying to bring the family together. She is the only one of us who ever really maintained a relationship with dad and she always updated everyone on what was going on in our lives. She protected Tomas and kept mom alive when we all abandoned her. I can't compete with that Jones; I hate her."

Jones took a breath in and tried not to laugh, "well brother, I have two suggestions for you, take them or leave them. First, I think you should seek some therapy for these deep seeded issues you have described to me here tonight. Second, try not to hate your dead sister too much, it's bad Karma."

Matthew stared at Jones knowing that he would crack. The two of them burst out laughing and Matthew conceded that his brother's advice was sound and may have some potential for the long term.

Katherine admired the soy growing in the field in front of her house; she put her empty glass down on the table in front of her rather than rising to fill it. Today she was uncharacteristically somewhat sober; she had been to her doctor in the morning to get more pills and she had known that he wouldn't appreciate her visiting drunk, and that she might get busted.

She looked at her arms, wrinkled and full of age spots, and wondered where her life had gone. She thought about her parents and the tumultuous relationship they had shared, as well as her marriages and the negative outcomes that spawned from them. She thought about Marie.

If she had opted not to have that child her life would have…could have been so different. Here she was, so alone, mildly comforted when thinking about her dead daughter and how life might have been if she had been dead as a fetus. Katherine decided that she needed another drink; the first one hadn't freed her mind of these tiring thoughts.

On her way in she passed by the side table where the mail was kept and something caught her eye, something Tomas must have missed when he brought it in. There was an envelope, addressed by hand, and the return mailing address merely said: Marie.

James walked through the market alone and hung over. His stomach longed for sustenance; his mind longed for meaninglessness. He touched fruit but felt no ripeness; he smelt the roses but they lacked aroma. He was empty and appreciated nothing.

He sat on a bench. He watched the people pass, ignorant of his heart ache, ignorant of his thoughts. James searched the crowd for something to distract him; he noticed a little boy wandering around alone. The child couldn't have been older than four and he appeared to be lost so James got up to approach him. He lost sight of the kid for a moment between the passing people but caught a quick look of the small blue overalls roaming away. James shuffled through the crowd trying to make his way to the boy.

A larger man bumped into him and James excused himself, assuming it to be his fault. He saw the boy again reaching for an orange from one of the stands about thirty feet in front of him. As he headed in that direction he heard a woman's voice call out nervously, "Marty…where are you baby? Marty!" He turned to see where the mother was calling from and as his eyes darted from the boy towards the direction of the voice, he caught a glimpse of Marie's smile walking through the crowd. He stopped dead and tried to recapture the sight. He scrolled the faces one by one desperately seeking her. He was reminded of his original task when he heard the mother yelling again, this time much more frantically.

He continued walking towards the boy but searching the crowds for her face. There she was, James could see the back of her head, and he recognized her wavy blond locks. He was now aggressively making his way through the crowd towards this vision. He pushed more people than he needed to but he wasn't going to lose her this time; he couldn't believe his eyes. He was a few feet away from her when his legs became entangled. He had fallen over the boy in blue, and the child was screaming. He stood up to find her but she was gone. After scanning the crowd one more time he then kneeled to be face to face with the boy and he patted the youth on his head and said, "I am not sure who is more lost".

As the boy calmed the mother found them in the crowd and quickly took her son in her arms, squeezing tightly and protectively. She looked James up and down, assumed by his handsome appearance that he was trustworthy, and walked away without saying a word; James noticed that she was wearing a sun dress that Marie had owned but that this lady didn't wear it as well.

He tried to remember the last time that the deceased had worn that white sundress but the harder he tried to remember the more it hurt him that he wasn't successful; he felt as if he was betraying her. He needed to leave this place, there was too much here. As he made his way out the exit he turned hoping that he would see her face in the crowd smiling at him; he turned to see the faces of a hundred strangers. He knew nothing of this loneliness; he knew nothing of this insanity.

"Are you sure this is where you want to be?" Kay asked protectively.

"What does that even mean?" the girl sat, arms crossed.

Kay was so angry with the girl that she couldn't even look at her. "Are these the faces you want to see? Do you want to look around at your friends and see your mother, a choice select few boys your age and me? Take a good look around you, are you sure this is where you want to be?

"Of course....this is where I am so why don't you think this is where I belong? Why don't you stop projecting your lost dreams onto me?" the girl said to her elder, knowing immediately that she had struck a nerve.

Kay turned towards her counter and weakly gripped the edge of it in frustration.

"I am not projecting. I am just taking notice that you were accepted into a respectable school in another country but you are choosing to stay here for reasons that I don't understand or that you just haven't shared with me." Kay took a hold of one of the wooden chairs in her kitchen and took a seat in it. "It hurts me that you can leave here and you don't."

"Just because I have the opportunity does not mean that I should do it."

"It is a waste if you do not go."

"But why? I have proven to myself that I am good enough to go, that I am good enough to be more. Why should I go to a place I don't know to prove something I don't appreciate?"

Kay could see what a mistake the girl was making and she shook her head in *disappointment;* her chest was convincing her to cry, and so she did. The young female admired this woman's passion for her future and so she continued calmly, "whether you believe me or not I am excited for my future. I just don't believe that I need to prove anything, and if I don't need to prove anything then why should I choose a future that I don't want? I will be successful. I will be happy. I don't need to run away in order to do these things. I am not you; I am me and I am happy with being unextravagant."

"But you don't know how good it could be."

"So why don't you accept that I could know on the path that I am taking?"

"Because it is the wrong path", her elder told her.

"Can I ask you a question?"

"Nothing has ever stopped you."

"Are you upset with my choice because you made a mistake when you were young or because you chose to go against the odds and you were happy with the outcome?"

The elderly figure turned her back to youth and thought intensely for a moment. She debated between truth and fiction and decided solidly on one of her choices before she turned back. The girl waited for the answer, though she was growing weary of this remnant of a conversation. Kay spoke, "I am happy that you are strong enough to make your own decisions despite the contradictions around you. I am happy that you are independent enough to know your options and make a choice. I am going to add though, that if you are basing your decision on a man then you are far less intelligent than I thought you were, and if I ever find out that this suspicion is true then I will use it as ammunition against you for as long as I know you. You are bigger than this place and you are better than most people, it would be an absolute tragedy to lose you to mediocrity."

The younger shook her head unacceptingly; she agreed about her potential and was resentful that her elder counterpart suspected the persuasion of a male presence, though it was insightful. She had only one thing left to say, "I should go", she said as she turned towards the door.

"Are you going because I am right or because I have offended you?" Kay asked.

"You have successfully done both of those things today, but I am surprisingly not impressed like I usually am. One might say that I am genuinely apathetic." She left the dated kitchen, seemingly antipathetic. The girl was frustrated, bitter, yet deep in thought, questioning her decision. The elderly woman was left alone smirking sinfully to herself, knowing that she had sparked a fire within a young girls mind.

Deep in fragmented thought Chris shuffled his stack of equation filled pages. He took a breath in and his conscious mind surfaced. He noticed the other five men sitting at the boardroom table staring at him awaiting his answer. "I wouldn't suggest that you leap into this deal without a thorough investigation. I will forward you my preliminary findings and we can meet again early next week to discuss the situation as I see it."

A grossly overweight executive sitting down the table from Chris inquired "Why don't you go over your assessment with us now Stephenson?"

Yearning to be finished with this deal he knew that he had to escape this recycled air and the assholes he was sharing it with, "No, I need to go….I have a prior commitment."

"This deal is worth millions to us, I suggest you reschedule your other commitment." The same obese man asserted as he wiped the sweat from his face with a tissue.

"Sorry Sam but I need to leave, the deal will be there on Monday… trust me….no one in their right mind would jump on this one." Chris packed his now neatly piled stack of spreadsheets into his briefcase for safekeeping and excused himself from the room. He smirked proudly as he reached for the door knob; he was finally following Marie's advice.

"You take work too seriously" Marie told him boldly.

"Well, little girl, I am trying to set an example for you. We can't all play games every day and have fun all the time."

"I hate when you call me little girl", She protested.

"You are a little girl to me."

"But I'm eighteen and I have a job just like you."

"Your age makes no difference to me, you will always be a little girl. And I wouldn't compare your job to mine just yet....though being a waitress is very respectable." He said mockingly.

"I'm a server by the way and you still take your work too seriously....I mean honestly...lighten up", she said playfully.

Chris chuckled at her simplicity and didn't give her comment a second thought. Moments later she continued with her advice as if he was listening intently. "Have you ever told your boss that you couldn't work on a weekend? Have you ever put your personal life before work? If I needed you could I ever feel confident that you would be there for me or would it depend on your next big deal? Do you even love your work?"

"You shouldn't ask too many questions at once if you ever expect an answer."

"They're not really questions, more like statements with a question mark at the end."

"You are a funny little girl." He pat her on the head lovingly and continued typing on his laptop quirkily with his two index fingers.

"I think you might be the funny one." Marie said. Then she stood up and kissed him on top of his head. "Someday you should just walk away from work and feel how liberating it can be....and don't call me little girl."

As Chris walked through the door he glanced back at the suits around the table so that they could see him smiling and they would know that he was different now.

When the door shut behind him one of the men left at the table quietly cleared his throat and took the liberty of sharing some privy information that his secretary had told him moments before the meeting. "Do you guys know where Stephenson went last week?"

"For vacation?" Someone guessed.

"Not quite…his daughter died…I heard she killed herself."

The larger man turned white. "Why wouldn't he tell us? He seemed so together?"

"Actually Sam, I think that may have been Christopher Stephenson undone."

Samson watched Marie stand at his kitchen counter as she gracefully chopped an onion. He admired her casual, elegant, comfortable beauty. When her eyes watered she wiped the tears on her aged wool cardigan, the French knife never leaving her hand; she looked over towards him and smiled at her false sadness. He loved her. She asked him to light a candle, claiming that the flame would subdue the fumes. He did as she asked and admired the flickering flame reflecting off of her bare neck. He wondered how to tell her without scaring her away; he was aware of her instant flight patterns. He believed that she felt the same way by the way she looked at him; she had cried when he cried; she had laughed when he had laughed.

"You are my best friend" he told her.

She looked at him curiously and admitted, "you are okay too I guess" as she laughed at her nonchalant answer.

Samson recognized her joke, "No. I am serious."

"So am I", she said.

Samson decided that now wasn't the time. He would hold out for the right occasion to talk about his idea for the future. Marie seemed to be a little too playful this evening; or she knew what he wanted to say and was very good at avoiding the conversation.

"Sam…are you still here man?" James questioned curiously.

"Oh yeah….sorry…I guess I zoned out there for a minute" Samson replied.

"Or two" James added.

"Yeah….sorry…what were you saying?" he asked not really caring for the answer.

James took a drink of his beer, "Nothing, I was just being my usual depressed self."

"I really am sorry man, I suck. Please go on, I didn't mean anything by it. I can only imagine how bad you are hurting right now."

James examined Samson's face to determine whether or not he was being sincere. He always wondered about them. "I just miss her" he admitted.

"We all do James" he tipped his beer up to his mouth and wondered while he drank. He knew he shouldn't, but he wanted someone else's opinion. "Why do you think she did it?"

James looked his company in the eyes and, though he desperately wanted to share, he merely uttered, "I don't know. What's your take on the situation? You knew her as well as any."

Samson dropped his head down and shook it in protest. He wanted to explain what he assumed her thoughts were but he felt as if he was over stepping his boundary. In frustration, James insisted, "come out with it, you wouldn't have asked if you didn't want to talk about it."

Samson thought about it and committed to his opinion, "She was always losing herself looking out a window, waiting for a war that she could revolt against. You know she was always waiting for more. I have never known anyone less content with just being. I think that she woke up one day and realized that there was nothing more; I think that's why she left. Better to choose a destiny then to wait for one that won't come." Samson, confident that he had hurt James by being right, took down some more of his ale. He sat and waited for a response.

James nodded his head in agreement. "She certainly did choose her own destiny." He waited a minute and then excused himself and headed for the washrooms downstairs wiping his tears as he walked away. Samson, trying to extract himself from reality, focused on the soap opera playing on the television hovering over the bar. The dialogue was simple yet complicated,

"Julie, how could you do this to me?" the handsome dimpled man asked desperately.
"Evan, how can you blame me? How could I help but fall in love with Jack?"
"You were never anything more than a tramp."
"How could you say that to me? I love you."
(pause) "I love you too Julie. Let's make this work." (the couple embraces passionately)

Samson was relieved by the commercial break and refocused on his beer. He pondered life for less than a moment and wondered what she was thinking now as she watched them.

"Marie, I have something I want to tell you. Something I need to tell you." Samson was speaking with a clear mind and an anxious heart.

She looked him honestly in the eyes and encouraged him "go on..."

"Well, I want to tell you something that you probably already know; something that I think you have been avoiding." She nodded with interest as he continued. "I...I love you. I want us to be together. I know that you love me and that we would be good together. I know your quirks and your faults and I love you still. You know me, we already share everything except a bed. We have the same sense of humor, and we have great conversations." Samson was starting to believe he was trying to convince her rather than admit to her. He paused long enough to get a reaction from her.

She shut her eyes momentarily as if thinking and she took in a deep breath as if to speak but nothing came out. Her eyes peaked out from their lids and her voice braved a sentence. "I love you too".

He knew by her tone that there was a 'but'.

"Sorry about that Sam, I haven't had a lot of control over myself lately." James said as he re-approached the table.

"No problem man, I don't think any less of you because you are human."

"Do you think we could get together later when I have myself a little more together? Maybe we could call Con and Lil and have dinner or something", James suggested.

"That sounds great, why don't you give us a call when you feel up to it", Samson said sympathetically.

The two men loosely embraced and James left the pub feeling worse than when he had arrived. He thought that being with one of her closest friends would ease some pain but in reality it did nothing more than remind him of her and how misunderstood she was.

Samson both hated and pitied James as he left the bar. He would never understand why she stayed with him so long or what it was about him that attracted her. More so, he couldn't let go of what he could have had with her.

Jane struggled at her door with purse in hand; her keys were hiding beneath her inhaler and didn't want to be found. When she made the discovery and opened the door she felt relief for the first time that day. There was something about getting home at the end of a long work day that comforted her in ways that she was starting to understand. Jane kicked her shoes off and made her way to the answering machine as she was accustomed to doing. Her stomach got butterflies when she saw the flashing red message light; she was easy to excite. Eagerly she pressed the oversized grey button to hear from the world for yet another day.

As she listened she went to the fridge to pour herself a glass of chardonnay. She heard her sister's voice, "Hey Janey, wanted to see how you are holding up. Give me a call if you want to go out or something." BEEP. Mike's voice chimed in, "Jane? Are you home yet, if you are then please pick up. Um, I need to tell you something so please pick up if you're there. Call me when you get this." BEEP Jane was put off by Mike's tone and picked the phone up to call him back as she heard Katherine's voice, "Jane….this is Marie's mom. I….I got a letter today….it's from Marie. Please call me. Did you get one? I am going to call James. Please call me." BEEP BEEP

Jane stood still staring at the machine sorting out the information that was so presented to her. As she debated who to call first the phone in her hand rang loudly, startling her. Her new debate was whether or not to answer the ringing phone in her hand. She answered, "Hello?"

"Jane, thank god." She recognized Mike's nervous voice.

She interrupted him, "You won't believe the message I just got from Marie's mom. She said…"

"Jane I need to talk to you about something, but you have to try not to freak out on me okay", Mike said nervously.

"If you cheated on me then now isn't the best time to tell me about it. I am kinda going through a lot of other shit right now and I just don't have the energy to deal with that."

"No babe, I don't tell you about my cheating because then I will have to stop it, this is something unrelated. This is about your friend."

"She sent me a letter", Jane said knowingly.

"How did you know?"

"Where is it?" she asked trying to contain her rage.

"I have it."

"WHY do you have it Mike?"

"I grabbed the mail last Friday on my way out and it has sat in the passenger's seat of my truck ever since. I leafed through it today and saw your letter. I will be home soon, I am sorry. How did you know though?" he asked again.

"I heard your message, I heard Katherine's message. I will see you when you get here." She was feeling quite bitter.

"It won't be more than five minutes."

Jane hung up the phone. She sat down at her desk and thought about what her girlfriend would say to her. She wondered what she herself would write if given one last chance to communicate with her lost friend. She came up blank.

When Mike swung open the front door she couldn't pretend that she wasn't waiting for his arrival. He held out the letter and Jane grabbed it from his hand without a shadow of a false hello. He knew the importance of Marie's note and wondered why she wasn't more upset with him.

He watched as she opened the envelope, took a deep breath, and took the paper out to read. He watched as she unfolded the letter with closed eyes, opened her eyes and focused on the message. Jane didn't look at the paper for more than a minute before she laughed, threw the paper on the floor, and walked out of the room. Confused, he followed her into the kitchen, and cornered her between the stove and the bathroom door. Jane looked at his handsome face and he admired her eyes as they welled up and she began to pout and tried not to cry. Within a moment she could no longer hold her tears back. He embraced her as she bawled.

The curiosity killed him but he dared not ask what Marie wrote in the letter, nor did he act as if he knew there was a letter at all.

Half an hour later Jane fell asleep on their bed in the fetal position, completely wrapped up in a comforter. He had to know.

Mike entered the dining room and stared at the paper strewn flagrantly on the floor. He tried to read it without touching it for reasons of remorse but his attempts were in vain. As he bent over to pick it up he thought that Jane would share this privy information with him anyhow, so he should feel no guilt for invading her privacy. He read the note; he looked at the picture attached to the paper. He put the sheet back exactly where he found it and snuck back into bed despite the time of day. As he admired Jane's flawless features, he smirked at the implications of Marie's post mortem enthusiasm and it was all he could think about as he tried to go to sleep that night.

So simple, so to the point, she couldn't have written it better. There was a Polaroid of Marie giving the finger with a face a pure satisfaction. She had attached this picture to a page on which she casually typed out "lighten up".

It was beautiful and Mike hadn't fully appreciated the deceased's sense of humor until this point. He laughed aloud in a moment of weakness and Jane stirred. His fear of waking her prevented him from any more outbursts. He wondered if the woman lying beside him would ever tell him what the letter said. What he didn't know is that she was awake the whole time and knew that he had snuck out to read it. The question was really, would she ever lighten up?

Lillian noticed her front door was ajar as she approached it. Curiously, she pushed it open and happily hopped up the stairs. At the top she was not overly surprised to find Connor sitting alone on their worn couch with a scotch in his left hand resting on his leg and, inquisitively, a hand written letter in his right. He didn't acknowledge her entry so she became even more intrigued with this bizarre situation.

To her dismay the intrigue transformed into anxiety when he turned to face her and uttered the words, "Marie wrote us a letter". Lillian went straight to the kitchen, poured herself around three ounces of scotch, and joined her husband on the couch. He passed the note over without a word; she didn't know what to expect. She and Marie had always enjoyed each other because they never knew what to anticipate from the other, and so, she read:

A letter for my brother and his wife, a dear friend of mine.

Connor, I want to thank you for teaching me to cook, to appreciate authors like Hesse and Robbins, and to tolerate a person so like myself. I know that you thought many things about me and that, more importantly, you loved me despite the fact that you couldn't stand me sometimes. Hesse wrote, "if you hate a person, you hate something in them that is a part of yourself. What isn't a part of ourselves doesn't disturb us." I know that you were disturbed by me because you feared that you were ill like me. I know that you said terrible things about me in order to restore confidence in yourself;

I only care that you loved me to my face. I want you to know that I have known you and your bitterness wholly and that I love you despite your attempted withdrawals. I suppose there is a positive to being slightly removed from reality; there is hesitation to accept it. I loved you and, if I can now, I will continue to. You are a good brother, and a better friend. Stop drinking in my name.

Lillian, there are too many things I want to say to you that I don't want my brother to read so I will keep it short and sweet. Dare I say, I couldn't have chosen a better partner for Connor had I tried. Nor could I have hand picked a better friend for myself. To keep in my tradition of using quotations instead of my own words I must now borrow the words of Hesse again, "some of us think that holding on makes us strong; but sometimes it is letting go." I write this only so that Connor will read it and know that it is fine that you two were laughing at my funeral. I love you because you inspire the positive from the negative and I love him because he most likely still feels guilty about my life. I know that you are privately mad at me for leaving you but I hope that you understand why I had to go. Life is rarely kind; even less so to the person who questions their existence. Thank you for encouraging me to question.

I love you both, and feel free to name your first born after me; any name will do as long as the thought is there.

Marie

Lillian took a deep breath and laid her head back against the couch with ease. She turned towards him and sighed, "I really miss your sister and her ridiculousness." Connor nodded yet said nothing. "Marie planned her death like women plan their wedding, to be original and memorable. So much so that it will be hard to shake her from your mind. I bet she still has more in store for us", Lillian said confidently.

Lillian hid her disbelief when her husband shed a momentous tear; it toured down his cheek and hung for a moment on his chin before losing its grip and exploding on his faded black led zeppelin shirt. As she admired her husband's conviction she hoped that he could learn from this situation. He needed to understand some things about himself and now was as good a time as any to start.

After some deliberation the couple agreed that receiving a letter from a dead girl was as good a reason as any to get shit canned and so, they did. That night they refused to accept any sort of truth that the deceased had communicated with them. They denied her very existence until the morning when they were forced to deal with both a hangover and the consciousness of spirituality and insight.

As the young girl took a sip of her tea she watched Kay rub her arms for warmth. "I don't mean to be rude, but can I ask how old you are?"

Kay made a face, "Why is that rude? Is my age something I should be ashamed of, or something I have cause to hide?"

The girl turned red with shame, "I'm sorry I just.."

"Oh never mind now, I am ninety-two and counting."

"Wow…that's impressive. You are really lucky that your health has been so good."

"Now if I ever teach you anything young lady, let it be this: don't tell someone that they are lucky unless you know them to be so. It is insulting to be told about my good fortune when you know nothing of my life or my hardships."

"I didn't mean…"

"It doesn't matter what you meant, it matters what you say and how I interpret it. That can be another lesson, but that is from my advanced class."

"Would you mind explaining to me why you are offended by me saying that your good health has been fortunate?" the girl asked defensively.

"Well dear, I thought you would never ask", was Kay's reply. "The most obvious in my mind is that I still think of myself as being your age, a beautiful young woman with a life ahead of her and an undetermined amount of futures before her. I am trapped in the body of an old woman. My mind has trouble understanding why my body won't move the way I want it to, I am limited to shuffling around this old house with difficulty. I look in the mirror and my gorgeous flawless skin is ragged, wrinkled and sagging; my bright smile has transformed into a permanent frown. I only recognize my eyes, but they look so tired. Where did my youth go?

I look to my past and am sick thinking about the people I have lost. My mother left me first, followed by my father and my siblings dropped one by one after that. My husband, the love of my life left me thirty years ago. I had two children, both died before me; that's not supposed to happen you know, parents are supposed to die first. All my friends from over the years are dead and their stories will die with me. I suppose you are the exception to that.

I look to the future and I feel dead inside knowing that my fate is sealed. I will bide my time wandering through this house and drinking tea until I get a cold that my old immune system won't be able to fight, it will turn into pneumonia and I will die in a hospital bed alone. There will be a write up in the paper but the only person that will cut it out will be your mom, knowing that you wouldn't have the foresight to look it up yourself.

I guess I don't really feel all that lucky. In fact I feel wronged by God, but that is a whole other can of worms I won't open today. Are you starting to understand why you shouldn't tell someone how lucky they are?"

The young girl was looking into the remains of her tea trying to think of an appropriate thing to say in such a situation. She realized that there was no such thing to say so she settled with, "I'm sorry".

"What on God's green earth are you sorry for girl?"

In a panic she scrambled for anything to come to mind, "I…am sorry that…I even asked about your age."

Kay looked her in the eyes inquisitively and smiled "Don't worry about it. You can't tell but I am very glad that you asked. When I am forced to say the things I think out loud it is easier for me to recognize how ridiculous I am." Kay sipped on her tea and noticed how uncomfortably confused the girl across the table was and so she added, "I was just trying to teach you a lesson."

The youth smiled with relief after she finished up her cold tea and she excused herself from the table and said her goodbyes. Kay was tired from her rant so was accepting of the girl's hasty exit.

On her walk home the girl concluded that their visits should be more frequent; there were some lessons in that old mind that may come in handy.

As he approached the graveyard, Tomas put his foot on the brakes, put the car into park and turned off the ignition. He looked over towards the headstones and then turned to his passenger and said, "well, here we are". James asked him if he was going to come but Tomas shook his head, "nope".

"Thanks for the ride, I shouldn't be long", James said with his hand on the door.

"Take your time; I brought a crossword to pass the time." He held up the puzzle as if to prove that he was fine with the situation. James nodded and got out of the car. He walked across the old country road and up the grassy knoll towards her body. Tomas watched him walk away with a single red rose in hand; he thought that James seemed nervously excited, like he was actually going to see her. He shook his head with pity and worked on 3 down.

James, wearing her favorite shirt of his, walked right up to her stone; this was his first time back since the burial. He sat down facing her lifespan carved into the grey stone and he looked up to the sky thinking she might make it rain but the sun was shining. He began, "I came here to read you a letter I wrote you. You always told me that I wrote well, so I thought you would like a letter. I named the letter 'learnings' which I think is improper English but it is creative so you might approve." He took the folded up paper out of his jacket pocket. He read it over once to be sure it was error free, he wouldn't want to disappoint her if she was listening.

"If I say to you that I haven't stopped thinking about you, it may be something you have heard a few times before from a few other men. I think that means at least one thing: you must have some incredibly amazing and truly undeniable qualities to make you so unique and desired. I think that anyone would agree with me on this point. This is what I have to say. It is a sort of beautiful fear to love you and that makes me think constantly about you, about being with you, but the conclusion stays the same, regardless of its beginning." James stopped for a moment. He was second guessing his flow and his atrocious grammar. He hoped that she would forgive him of those faults because of the heartfelt content.

"I learned that you like one ice-cube in your soup, Beef Tenderloin is the only meat you eat and only with red wine. I learned that you are the saddest person alive at times but, when you are happy, you are the happiest person on earth, and that when you feel that way you jump on the bed in the morning and sing "I love my life!"

I learned that I loved to be there as the future unfolded in front of us because there was no other place like that. I learned that I shouldn't breathe on you in bed at night because it prevents you from sleeping and that your naked body will haunt my dreams for as long as I will have dreams.

I learned that caffeine and gluten are not your friends, so I made them my enemies. I learned that you are neither superior nor perfect, but that you are simply a woman (maybe not a simple woman). I learned what love is, and what that meant in my life, especially now that you are gone.

I learned that Hazel was going to be the name of our daughter, and Christian our son, that we will have a big dog and that no one will ever take this dream from me. I have no sad memory of you; just the way you wanted. My memories of you will always be with me, making me smile like no other woman could ever make me smile. My pure love for you remains untouched as it was the day that I first felt it, with no sadness or remorse, just joy that I can feel it still."

James put the rose down on her grave and freely wept. "I will never smell another flower without envisioning it in your hair." He knew that his crying would make her feel awkward so he helped himself up and walked away. He felt a chill as he walked across the street and he hopped back into the car with Marie's little brother.

"How did it go?" Tomas asked casually.

"I feel better having said it but I don't feel the relief that I thought I might", James said.

Tomas put the car into drive and waited for a car to pass before he could pull out. "I doubt that she will ever leave us completely James. Most things remind me of her still."

James smiled at him, "that's funny Tom because you don't seem overly affected by the loss."

Tomas, straight faced, turned his attention back to the road and said, "that's not our way, you should know that."

As the two pulled away, a drop of rain fell from the sky and landed on to the windshield, a small indication of the storm that followed.

A Cat Power c.d. played quietly in the background, "*I do believe, in all the things you see. What comes is better than what came before.*" Jones sat uncomfortably in the middle of a room on his hardwood floor. He held his knees to his chest and stared at a piece of scrap metal. It was the first time in his life that he sat before raw materials and struggled for the perfect concept to come to mind. As the local newspaper affirmed, "He was a recognized artist with undeniable original talent," yet he sat here listening to a c.d. his sister had made him, thinking about his subject and nothing was coming to his heart or mind. He focused back on the music, "*What comes is better than what came before.*"

He thought about Marie, though she was ten years younger than he, the two had more in common than any of them. They both loved art and had some talent, they both were melancholic borderline alcoholics with horrendous smelling feet and people were drawn to them both in ways that even they didn't understand. Jones felt as if he didn't deserve to miss her. He lived farther away than the rest of the brothers and rarely took the chance to visit, but when he did the two were never at a loss for words.

He sank his head into his hands. He looked around at his empty apartment and he, in turn, felt emptier. Marie always told him that she envied him and his living conditions; she wished that she could be separated from her possessions and the importance that they held. He could never really tell if she was serious or sarcastically mocking him. As his mind wandered, he stumbled upon an idea, Jones knew just what to do but he was going to need more materials.

He started working. After an hour his shirt met the floor; an indication that this was going to be a long night. Jones didn't take a break for the next fifteen hours. He had friends come by with more scrap materials.

When he finished he stood back and admired his work. He sat down, picked up his phone and dialed his brother's number.

"Hello?" Connor answered.

"Connor, it's finished." Jones said casually concealing his excitement.

"Already?" Connor asked in disbelief.

"Yep. It looks pretty good but we may fall into one problem."

"What's that?" the younger brother asked.

"It may be impossible to get it out of my apartment", he said laughing.

"That sounds like a challenge. I will be right over." Connor said eagerly.

"Give me time to sleep."

"I'll call you in six hours", Connor said.

"Bye."

Jones hung up the phone and looked up at his work. It was easily the most beautiful thing that he had ever made. He smiled and, knowing that she was listening, he said "thank you". He grabbed a pile of his clothes from a corner and piled them up as a pillow; when you don't own a bed, any floor will do. He recalled the last time that he had declared a piece of art his best.

"Okay come in but it's not done yet…there is lots of work to do on it still", Jones told his sister hesitantly.

"Don't worry….I am not that judgmental. Where is it?" she asked.

"It's in the living bedroom. Do you want something to drink?"

"Yes please…whatever will do."

Marie wandered into the living room while Jones poured her a glass of water. He was nervous following her in and wondered what she would think. He had convinced himself that he didn't care what she would think but was currently reconsidering his original acclamation.

When he entered the room he saw that she was crying. "I titled the piece 'sunset'." He approached her trying to seem nonchalant and passed her the glass.

She wiped the flagrant tear from her face and told her brother honestly, "this is the most beautiful piece of work you have done yet". He smiled and nodded in agreeance but said nothing for fear of seeming pompous in front of his ever so seemingly simple sister.

She sat down in front of his metal creation and did nothing but admire it for what seemed like an hour before she realized the time and she got up again and told him how amazing he was, just to walk out the door without so much as a good bye. He knew from that day forward that she understood what he was about. She proved that day that she could appreciate the sadness in his art as no one else could. His piece was titled after the always beautiful sunset but his sister cried when she saw it; Marie had seen the darkness in his art that no one else could.

His head faced the sunset as he lay on a large pile of dirty clothes that doubled as a cot. He wondered if his sister would be lying in bed right now thinking of him if he had died. He considered her death and how dramatic it was. It seemed she made an art of dying; her final work. Jones tossed a few times before he fell asleep in his unconventional uncomfortable bed with comforting thoughts of a manic depressive dancing in his head.

Katherine smashed around the kitchen trying to find something to drink. She had one of the kitchen cupboards open and was reaching her hands up with difficulty to feel around for a hidden bottle on the top shelf. She could feel it on the tip of her finger and reached with all her ability to get a hold of it. She grasped the tip of the bottle and relaxed down onto her heels. As she pulled it out of the cupboard she lost her grip and fumbled with it until she fell and the bottle smashed on the floor.

Katherine wept as she lifted herself to her knees. Tomas heard the commotion and came in to her aide but didn't rush. He saw the mess and warned her not to move while he left to get the broom. Frustrated, she tried to pick up the pieces and sort them into a pile. Tomas returned and yelled, "stop helping". She wiped her tears on her sweater sleeve. He noticed her crying and felt enraged, "are you crying because you hurt yourself or because you just broke your only way to continued intoxication for the night?"

"Shut up" she snapped back while continuing to try to pick up the shards of glass.

"If you don't stop touching the fucking glass I will walk away and let you do it all yourself. Would you like that?" he asked aggressively.

Katherine shot a raging glare at her son. She picked up the neck of the bottle and threw it at Tomas with every effort she was capable of giving. The jagged edge caught him on his left arm just above the elbow. His pasty white skin was quickly smeared bright red.

He looked at her in shock before he yelled, "Unfuckingbelievable!" He tossed the broom in her direction and ran to the washroom. He grabbed a white towel and wrapped it securely around his wound. He listened to his mother flustered in the kitchen trying to clean up her mess while he watched the blood slowly soak through the towel. He noticed the drops of blood leading to where he sat. It reminded him of another bloody floor; though the one from his memory was far more flooded. Tomas tried to determine whether or not the nausea he was feeling was from his current condition or the recall of Marie bleeding out.

He moved over to the toilet and sat back with his eyes shut trying to figure out what to do but his thoughts kept focusing back to that day when she tried to end it.

Marie was unconscious when he found her. There was blood pooled around her. Her dress was white where it wasn't blood soaked and her skin wasn't far from matching. Tomas stood in the doorway of his sister's bedroom for what seemed like minutes staring at the bloody mess in front of him before he realized that she may not be dead. He didn't call out to his mother for fear that Marie could be dead. He knelt beside her, knees in her blood and leaned over her with the intention of checking her pulse. With his face so close to hers he could hear her breathing and so, he panicked. He screamed, "mom....mom.....call 911...call 911". He tried to wake his sister by slapping her face.

Katherine ran into the room in horror and somewhat calmly started directing her son. She ran back downstairs to the phone and dialed while Tomas grabbed some white hand towels from the bathroom. He tied them tightly around her wrists. Katherine yelled up the stairs, "stay with her Tom, they want me to stay on the phone, don't leave her alone." He lightly slapped her face a few more times to try and wake her but she didn't move. He gently crossed her arms across her stomach and he slid his pubescent arms underneath her neck and knees. He lifted her up, talking to her the entire time, and carried her downstairs so that the paramedics wouldn't have as far to go in order to help her. He slid at first in the blood that had gathered on the hardwood floor but regained control and proceeded with caution. He carried her right outside and onto the grass. Katherine couldn't stand it any longer; she hung up the phone and followed her children outside.

Fearful, she knelt beside her son and took a piece of her daughter's bloodstained skirt into her palm and held onto it as if it were Marie's hand. She didn't shed a single tear nor did she come undone as they waited for help. Tomas admired his mother that day for being as strong as she needed to be; he always compared her to the magnificent person that she was on that day. He had been disappointed ever since.

Tomas was awakened from his trance when his mother stumbled into the bathroom. "You need to respect me", she affirmed.

"Whatever", was all he could muster as a reply.

"Are you okay?" Katherine asked as she let out a hiccup and used the door frame to support her weight.

"I am fine; it wasn't deep enough to do any permanent damage like death", he said sarcastically.

"Was that supposed to be funny?" she asked trying to focus her eyes without shutting one.

"It wasn't supposed to be anything mom, just go to bed."

Katherine decided to end the conversation so she turned around, guiding herself with her hands against the door frame. She mumbled as she walked away, "I demand respect. This is my house. You kids never treat me right." When Tomas could no longer hear her he snuck into the kitchen, feeling a little woozy, to call Connor to perform some first aid.

When he walked in to the room he stepped on the broken glass that apparently wasn't quite cleaned up and fell in pain. Upon examining his socked foot he saw that he now had a second bloody wound. He paused for a moment feeling frustrated and he laughed hysterically. He looked up at the ceiling and managed to blurt out, "I know you are watching this, I hope you had nothing to do with it or you will pay". Tomas figured Marie would have planned for him to hurt his foot so he would see the humor in all of this.

He reached up for the phone and dialed Connor; he was getting drunk at Jones' so Lillian came in his place.

When she arrived, she cleaned the glass from the floor and dealt with the wound.

"Thank you for coming" Tomas said to his sister in law.

"My pleasure little brother. Plus I promised Marie I would take care of you in her absence."

"You knew that she was going to leave?" Tomas asked curiously.

"Not exactly," she explained, "Marie left me a cheat sheet on how to take care of your family. It's hard to explain but the answer to your question is no, I didn't know she was going to leave. Why don't we talk about something a little less depressing?"

The two of them discussed a range of topics from Freeman's fear to face his children to the curiousness surrounding Jones' empty apartment. She put Tomas to bed after a half an hour as he had lost enough blood to need some sleep.

While her husband developed a not so cunning plan to extract a large piece of art from a dilapidated apartment across town, Lillian cleaned up the mess in the washroom and thought about Marie's last day alive.

Marie pulled into her favorite sushi restaurant, her mouth was watering. It had been quite a while since she had the ambition to go out. As she walked along the mirrored windows she admired her reflection, this time feeling a little sad about how long she had let herself look any other way.

A man just ahead of her opened the door for her and she thanked him politely while secretly hoping he would check her out as she passed him by; he didn't, but she was ignorantly content not knowing. The Japanese host bowed as she entered and in perfect English he welcomed her, "It has been a long time Ms. Marie, how are you?"

"I am good", she replied with a smile, "how is school going Hiro? Are you the head of the class yet?"

"Of course I am," he laughed, "I am Asian remember!"

Marie chuckled, "of course you are, what was I thinking?"

The gentleman who had opened the door for Marie was behind them and growing irritable as his wait was lengthened by their conversation;

he cleared his throat to remind them he was waiting. The two turned towards him and smiled politely, Hiro acknowledged him, "How many in your group sir?"

"Just one", he answered with irritation in his voice.

"Well", the friendly host said, "I will be with you as soon as I seat this lady in front of you". Marie tried to hold back the smile but it wanted out, she had a habit of laughing at people like this man; people who didn't even have the patience to let two people reconnect. She used to be just like him. "Is it a table for two?" he asked her stepping back into his role.

"Yes, for two" she replied.

Hiro slowly walked her to the table chatting about school and life and placed her in the back corner, like he used to. She thanked him and watched as he approached the angry man to seat him.

Marie set the menus aside because she knew it by heart and pulled her notebook out of her purse. She was finishing up the list for Lillian. When her sister in law entered the restaurant Marie waved to get her attention and she stood to give her a hug. The two commented on how nice the other looked and after some quick chatting. Lillian noticed that Marie's skin was as white as the dress she was wearing.

Marie couldn't wait any longer. "Lil, I don't mean to start our lunch off heavily but I need to discuss some things with you."

Lillian put the menu down nervously as her friend was never so straight forward with her or in such a rush. She looked at her friend, pale and thinning still, and asked, "what is it that brings us here today Marie? Does it have anything to do with your health?"

Marie smiled, knowing very well how cleverly Lillian was trying to guess the purpose of this talk. "You will know soon enough Lil." Marie ripped a few pages of paper out of her note book and handed them over to her dear friend. "These are for you, let's call these pages, 'things to not let other people do', you will understand them more in a few days so please don't read through them until you know you are supposed to."

Lillian neatly folded the pages and put them into her purse with no intention of reading them until she knew to. "What's going on Marie?"

"Lil, could you imagine looking at Connor and knowing that you will never have children together; knowing that you will never have his babies and grow old together? Could you ever live knowing that one of you would have to live without the other?" Marie turned to Hiro who had returned to the table and she ordered for the two of them.

"Please tell me what is going on." Lillian pleaded with her, trying not to cry.

Marie, noticing a tear falling from her friend's face, started to well and answered, "I have come to a wall in my life that I cannot climb."

Lillian smiled, "what the fuck is that supposed to mean?" The two of them laughed.

"I don't know", was the reply. Marie looked over and saw some bowls approaching so she announced, let's talk less and eat more."

Lillian watched from across the table for the remainder of the meal as Marie laughed and talked about the weather and other non-important aspects of life. The two ate until they might explode and fought over who would pay the bill like good friends always do. Lillian let things go because she knew that Marie would explain what was going on when she was ready to. She thought about the list in her purse but accepted that she couldn't know what it was until she was supposed to.

The two women stood and walked each other out the doors. Marie stopped and stood beside Lillian for a minute or so before she held out her arms for a hug. The two embraced and as they parted Marie said to her friend, "You are the only one who can keep them all together."

"Keep who together?" Lillian asked.

"All of them Lil. I can't do it anymore so you need to."

Lillian laughed as she continued to walk away, "at least you aren't being creepily cryptic Mar!"

"Say hi to Connor for me." Marie yelled down the street as she got into her car. Before she put the keys in the ignition she sat and thought if there was anything that she might have missed. She pushed her hair behind her right ear and then turned the key, it was time to go.

As he woke, James opened his tired eyes; his body lay dead still. He looked around their room. His room. He shut his eyes to hide the truth. It had been a couple months since she died and her sloppy and chaotic messes were still everywhere. He had to start cleaning her stuff up; today would be the day. Knowing this was on the day's schedule, James went back to sleep.

When he woke for the second time that day, James opened his tired eyes and stretched out his long body. He sat up quickly, leaned back on his bed and scoped out his challenge for the day. Her laundry was still in and around the hamper; her half finished painting still stood upwards on her easel with paint tubes scattered on the table beside it; there were still remnants of their last intimate moments on the bedding; and her bobby pins were here, there and everywhere. James didn't want to let go of these things but he had been told numerous times by various people that living like this was very unhealthy. He agreed sometimes.

He hopped out of bed and put a coffee on before he started tidying up her painting station; he figured that this would be the easiest to start with. When he first approached the canvas he put his fingers on the paint to feel it; it became evident to him that the paint had not dried yet. He laughed at her love of slopping excess paint onto a canvas. His laugh quickly faded and he was left again with the pain of withdrawal.

Generally speaking, she always wrote when she was low and she always painted when she was high. He could remember her smile and the way she would bounce. He could remember her as if she had just left the room.

On his way home from work James felt worn-out and wondered what would be waiting at home for him. Instead of waiting to find out he took his cell phone out of his pocket and dialed her number. The phone rang four times and then went into voicemail. He began to dial again but ringing interrupted him; she was returning the missed call. He smiled, shaking his head and answered the call, "Hey beautiful."

"Hi, sorry I missed your call, I was painting", Marie explained.

"That's okay, how is the painting coming?"

"Alright. I think that you'll really like it. But you have to spend a couple minutes and look up close to really see everything", she said with excitement, "you'll see when you get home. Are you off yet?"

"I am two minutes away."

"Well then I'll see you soon. I want to finish what I am doing okay?" she said as she disconnected.

He hung up the phone and placed it back in his pocket. *She was in a good mood*, he thought to himself, what a relief. He unlocked the door and ascended to their apartment three floors up. As he walked in he heard the music playing loudly in the bedroom. He didn't bother announcing his arrival because she wouldn't hear him. She emerged from the bedroom wearing the jeans that he just bought her and one of his sweaters, both covered in paint. He took a deep breath to hold inside any potential anger he might feel when he noticed that she was smiling; he opted to accept the paint covered clothing as collateral damage. She ran to him and threw her arms around his neck.

"Are you excited to see it?" she asked.

"I really am. Maybe I should take a shower first so that I feel comfortable and clean when I see it the first time."

"Will it be a fast shower?" she asked anxiously.

"Five minutes", he assured her.

"Okay be quick." She tapped him on the bum as he walked towards the bathroom. James walked through the kitchen and noticed the dishes piled high and unwashed. He saw that the kitty litter was full, as well as the garbage. In the bathroom he picked up her pajamas on the tile floor from the morning. *She had to walk by these things a hundred times today*, he thought. He showered, dried himself and dressed in his track pants.

He left the bathroom for the bedroom to admire her latest work of art. He sat down in front of her painting. She spoke nervously, "Before you say anything, look at it for a few minutes, really take it in."

"I really like your use of colour", he said.

"Thank you."

"This reminds me of another artist."

"Van Gogh" she replied.

"Yes that's the one."

"That's who inspired me to do this one, with the swirls and the colours."

"I love it! I really love it! Where would you like to hang it?"

"Well it has to dry for a couple days before we hang it."

"Are you sure? We can't hang it right now? I just want it up on a wall." He mimicked her mania.

"Thanks honey, I knew that you would love it."

James took her in his arms and squeezed her as tight as he could. He found the spot on her forehead where she always parted her hair and he kissed her softly, leaving behind traces of his saliva. She pushed him away quickly and ran screaming through their apartment; he recognized this game and chased her. She turned around before he caught up to her and started patting her elbow so that he could see her and started to chant, "Elby is getting mad. Elby thinks that you deserve a visit."

He immediately changed directions and ran away in fake fear towards the bedroom laughing. She followed him in hysterics tapping her elbow and continuing the chant. As soon as he collapsed on the bed he placed his body in the fetal position and cried convincingly for help. She hurled herself on top of him and blew her elbow into his side and then his shoulder. She yelled excitedly, "Elby isn't satisfied…Elby needs more."

She kept slamming her elbow into his legs, his side and his biceps. Eventually, when he regained control of his outburst of laughing, he turned around and overpowered her and flipped her on her back in order to regain control of the situation. She giggled and admitted defeat while he admired her laugh. They made eye contact and he leaned down to kiss her; their lips met but their eyes remained open watching each other momentarily while they shared this moment. This kiss turned into that one and the next. He reached his hand up her shirt and took her breast in his hand. She moaned quietly and he pressed harder, fondling her nipple between his two fingers.

He whispered in her ear, "I love your body."

"I know baby, but ….."

"But what?"

"I really don't feel like it right now okay?" She slightly retracted from his embrace.

"You don't feel like me admiring your beautiful body?"

"No. I don't feel like where you admiring my body leads", she laughed.

"Seriously?" he asked.

"Yeah, sorry. I am really tired." She said imitating a tired person.

"Okay."

"Thank you", she said.

"Are you going to sleep now then?" he inquired.

"Maybe."

"Have you taken your pills?"

"No."

"Well you are definitely going to need some sedatives on top of your regular medication tonight otherwise no one will be sleeping." James reached to their bedside table and grabbed her pillbox while she changed into her unpainted pajamas. He emptied two chalky white pills, one large blue and red capsule and one tiny pink pill into his hand and replaced the lid on the container as she got into bed. He took the glass of water from next to the bed and handed it to her; she sat up.

"I hate taking those", she said.

"It is no big deal. Just the doctor's orders," James said with a loving smile.

"Do you know how nice it will be when I don't have to take any pills? When I will be free of people telling me that I am not right the way I am and that taking these ridiculous pills makes me more like everyone else.

Do you know how great it will be when I don't have to listen to doctors telling me how mentally and physically unhealthy I am?"

James smiled though his heart was breaking because he knew he had to say the truth, "Marie, you know that will never happen. You know that I will be handing you your pills for the rest of your life and you are going to fight me every step of the way."

"I do know that James." She pouted, "it is just nice to think about; a life without flaws."

"I think you are beautiful. I think you are perfect. I love your flaws; if we can call them that". James smiled honestly as he gave her the first pill and watched her force herself to swallow it. She shook her head back and forth quickly as if it were a struggle to get the small pill down. Marie took the second pill from his hand and placed it delicately on the back of her tongue for round two and repeated this again. She returned the glass to him and he got up to refill it because she always got thirsty throughout the night.

He leaned over her and kissed her on her hairline in his favorite spot and said lovingly,

"Goodnight Marie". He loved nothing more than saying her name out loud.

"Night buddy." She let out before rolling over.

Once he believed she was asleep, which didn't take long, he turned the television on to help him relax. Once he found a suitable show, he slowly curled into bed beside her but was careful not to wake her. This was a good day.

James smiled as he put her cadmium red paint right back from where he picked it up. He wasn't ready to disrupt her blissful chaos yet. He spent their life together trying to make her even but now that she was gone he couldn't let go of her odd. These pieces of her were going to fade in time with or without his help; it would be without his help. He chose to remember for as long as he could keep a grip on her.

He heard his kettle boiling and ran out to the kitchen. He didn't think about Marie again that day, any more than twenty times.

There was a light knock at the door which woke Kay. She had meant to only rest for a second until the pain subsided but she recognized that more time than that was lost as she tried to decipher the hour. The knock repeated at the front door, a few feet from her resting spot. She struggled to get up from the old awkward couch and moved as fast as she was capable, a brisk shuffle, towards the door.

As she opened the door she saw the girl making her way down the steps. She was wearing a yellow sundress instead of her usual masculine attire and she was carrying a bunch of lilacs in her right hand. Her blond hair was shining like the sun, though it was frizzy and sloppily thrown back in a ponytail. Quite striking, Kay thought to herself before asking, "Where do you think you're going?"

"I didn't think you were home", the girl replied.

"Well you need to give me a moment, I am not a jumpy teenager you know."

"Sorry. I tried the door but it was locked. So I assumed you must have been out."

"Do you ever know me to be out?" Kay asked.

"Sorry."

"Well get up here. What are the flowers for?"

The girl held them out to her. "I cut them for you from a tree out back of my house."

"Thank you that was very nice of you. Did your mother tell you to do it?"

"No she didn't. She did suggest that I wear this dress though. She has friends coming over later and she wants me to make an impression."

"You are old enough now that you don't have to listen to everything your mother tells you. You know that right."

"I know that, but it doesn't change much. I owe her too much not to give into the small things that make her happy."

"Well what you think you owe her is another story....set those flowers down and sit yourself down. Not on the steps with that dress on, sit up here on the porch in one of these chairs." Kay sat down in her usual rocker. She looked down the street; it was remarkably empty for such a beautiful day. "I wonder where everyone could be."

"Almost everyone is at church I bet." She replied swinging awkwardly on the porch.

"It's Sunday, yes, you're right. Why might I ask aren't you at church?"

"Mom gave up on me a long time ago and plus I learn a lot more from you then I do from Father Boreme."

Kay beamed with pride; she felt the exact same way. She looked down at the lilacs and reached for them with little intention of reaching them. The girl arose to pick them up for her and placed them gently in her hands.

Kay shut her eyes and ever so slowly brought the flowers to her nose. She inhaled deeply and the girl knew that she was triggering a memory. She always smelled things to remember better days, it was quite remarkable. The elderly woman's smile transformed to a grimace as she dropped the flowers and tightly gripped her stomach. The youth rose quickly and approached her. "Are you okay? What's wrong? Should I call someone?" Kay's pain diminished and her face returned to her normal calm demeanor.

"I am fine. I think that I ate some bad bread with my lunch this afternoon. I always forget how long things have been in the fridge."

"Are you sure", she asked nervously, "it looked much worse than some cramping."

"In old age people exaggerate to get attention. It must be imbedded in me by now. Sit down, give me some space, I am fine."

She did as she was told and sat back down in her chair. She waited watching to see if the hard woman in front of her was going to reveal another weakness but there was nothing. So she asked, "What were you thinking about when you smelled the flowers?"

The smile returned to Kay's face as she recalled. "I was remembering a time so long ago; a life time ago. I was a few years older than you are now and I was completely in love. I wanted to do something special for him, something that he would never forget." Kay paused and reached down to pick the flowers up to smell them again. "I loved lilacs more than any other flower and wanted him to have the same affectionate love for them as I did. I wanted him to be able to smell them and feel love as I did."

"Who? Your husband?"

"I am talking about the only man I ever really loved" Kay said without answering the question and the girl knew not to pry. "Well, to make a long story short, I spent an entire day while he was at work cutting the most beautiful lilac bunches I could find. I broke into his house and I arranged them all over, in the kitchen, bathroom, bedroom, everywhere I could. It took me hours but his whole house was perfumed with the lilac bouquets. He came home after work and found me there surrounded by all those gorgeous flowers. I jumped into his arms and we had one of the most wonderful kisses I can remember."

"So it worked!?"

"For the most part it did. Though he didn't care in the least about his broken window we had a minor disagreement about me taking all the flowers from the church. In the end we laughed about that."

"You took all those flowers from the church? Did you get in trouble?" she asked sitting on the edge of her swing.

"Not enough that is wasn't worth it. You should try that in your life if you have the chance. Do something sometime despite the repercussions but only when you will gain more from the action than you will lose. Make it a good story for others to listen to when you get old."

"You are a funny woman. Who knew you were such a badass back in the day."

Kay smiled but felt the pain returning. She was finding it harder and harder to be strong. The girl's attention was focused on the road at the moment so the elder took advantage of the situation. "I am going to lay down for a nap, why don't you head home and we can get together another time. Say hello to mother." Before the girl could stand her older counterpart was already inside with the door shut. Strange, she thought but she didn't reflect on it. She sat for a few minutes watching the quiet street and thinking before she got up to leave. She stood, fixed her dress, and picked up the lilacs from the floor where they rested. She set them down on the rocker, not wanting to disturb a woman on a mission to nap.

She walked home watching the people coming home from church and she laughed at the thought of a priest coming outside to be horrified at the sight of his pillaged lilac bushes. This uplifting thought would get her through dinner. She glowed as she walked down the street towards her home for an afternoon of being something that she wasn't.

Charles strolled through the market with his groceries searching for the perfect piece of cheese. He couldn't decide between blue cheese and Gouda, two very different cheeses he admitted to himself but both bring a lot to the table. As he picked up and put down a various number of aged cheese a woman knocked into him and he dropped one of his bags on the concrete floor. Before he could pick it up himself the lady bent over to rescue his lost vegetables. She raised her head and passed him the bag. He took a step back when she apologized and smiled in his direction. She was very pretty but it wasn't that that reminded him of Marie; it was her short black hair.

"Would you rather live a dying life or lose a life that was full?" Marie asked staring her assessor in the eyes.

Charles stared back at her feeling uncharacteristically awkward. He said nothing knowing that the silence would kill her and she would break it. He said nothing because his answer wasn't something you should say to a patient.

She predictably broke the silence, "I don't know, I guess I am being stupid."

Charles thought she was the most self-aware patient that he had. "Why would you say that you are being stupid?" he asked.

"Because you didn't answer my question, so I assumed it was dumb", she answered honestly.

"You need to stop judging your actions by how others see you. Do you ever form an opinion on what you do that is not based on what another might think?" He asked her knowing very well that she was completely dependent on judgment which is why she was so brutally judgmental herself.

"What are you but how others see you? You can tell yourself that you are something but if others don't see that then you are lying to yourself. I can tell myself that I am insecure and introverted but if I act outgoing and cocky whenever I am around people than that is what they will define me as."

"Do you believe that you are the 'cocky' person that others see or that you are the insecure person that you know you are?" he asked.

"Dr. Birmingham…..the only reason that you think I am insecure is because that's what I let you see. You are my doctor, I am your patient, did you ever think that I let you see what I think you want me to be? The truth is that I can be anything to anyone…but what does that make me? Am I everything or nothing? Am I this or that? Is there even a definable me?"

Charles sat back in his seat and pretended to write something down. He questioned whether she could actually lead him on about her personality. He paired her sense of duality with his diagnosis and felt more confident for a moment. He came up with a question, "So do you think that people only get from you what you want to give them? Do you think you have that much control or do you just wish you did?"

Marie sat on the couch pensively, drying her wet hands on her jeans. She knew what she wanted to say but she was searching for a clear and concise way of saying it. "Let me put it this way. When I lay in bed next to the man I love and he kisses me and we laugh together and we hold each other, I feel close to him but my chest feels tight because I feel like I have deceived him. He will never know me. I love him completely but he only loves this person that I have designed for him. I know he sees pieces when I let my guard down but I am a deceiver, I don't know how to be anything else. So yes, I do have that much control and I wish I didn't.

Yes I think that people only get from me what I want to give them."

Charles sat in his chair writing in point form the words that she had spurted at him. When he finished he looked at her and waited. He waited a little longer than usual for her to break the silence as she always did. He looked into her eyes and she just looked right back at him confidently. She had no intention of speaking and this disappointed him; this pissed him off. She was doing something completely uncharacteristic and it was eating him up that there might have been some truth to her bold acclamation of a completely counterfeit personality.

He felt angry with her and wanted to scorn her, so he asked, "why did you cut your pretty long blond hair and dye it black?" Charles immediately regretted asking and he was overcome by guilt as he watched her hold back her tears.

"You don't like it?" She asked as she touch the ends of her hair. Charles knew that she butchered her hair and compromised her beauty as a substitute for slitting her wrists. He looked at her squirming in her seat and answered her, "you look lovely", believing that if he didn't that she might go home and start slicing. The truth was that he knew one thing about this girl: she knew nothing of herself without others to judge her.

"I am going to grow it out again though" she said knowing what her new length inferred, "I will let it grow until I have to cut it again". Charles nodded so she would see his understanding, he looked at his watch and she started to put her coat back on.

"Do you need another prescription" he asked.

"No I'm good for a while."

"Are you sure because sometimes you miss appointments…I will just write you one now just in case you need it."

"Okay" she said waiting to get off of his uncomfortable fake leather couch.

He scribbled off a script and passed it to her. She took it from his hand and when she put her hand on the door handle she paused, turned back to him and said "I lied to you earlier. James knows me. James knows me and he loves me despite me, he sees all of my good." She didn't smile which Charles took note of and when he thought she had left she poked her head back into his office and stated "my family knows me too for the most part, but they hate me. They only want to see my bad I think." Now, with a wily grin, she left and shut the door behind her. He smiled, noticing the pattern that she always made a clever exit.

Charles found himself dumbly standing in a busy market place with a piece of Swiss cheese in his hand. He looked at the holey dairy and decided to buy it. Sometimes you need to let go of what you think you want, especially when there is a decision to be made.

Connor knocked at the door; this was a drop in visit but he knew James was home because he wasn't at work. There was no answer so he tried the handle. The door was locked so he tried the key that Marie had given him for safe keeping. The door opened in and Connor could smell from the second he entered that James was smoking and drinking himself to unconsciousness.

He verified this as he entered the living room to the sight of the man sprawled out shirtless on the couch; his gurgling half snore is what gave his drunkenness away. Connor kicked his friend's legs to rouse him, "get up" he said as a warning. "Get up!" he repeated as he picked James' legs up and swung them around onto the floor.

As James came to, he realized who was sitting down beside him and lighting one of his smokes. The groggy half drunk sat up and gave Connor a nod hello as he collected his thoughts and realized his whereabouts. Connor got up and walked to the kitchen to grab two beers. James knew that alcohol was coming his way but dreaded it as he was holding back from vomiting as it was; he had trouble saying no to Connor, he always had. He took the opened beer from Marie's brother who wore a suspicious smile. Connor began, "today is the day that you forget about her".

James was irritated by this comment but let out a chuckle, "I doubt that will be as easy as you think."

"Jump in the shower", Connor insisted. "We are going for a walk, and then we will grab something to eat."

James thought about it for a minute before he remembered his inability to deny this man of anything he asked, "I will go, but I won't shower."

"Trust me dude, shower."

James showered; all the while dreading the outcome of this day. He put a sweater on and then he and Connor hit the street. "So where are we headed?" Connor, like always, was ambiguous; "this way" he said telling him nothing. The inappropriate conversation to follow was everything James expected and more. "So how long are you planning on staying miserable?" Connor asked calmly. James noticed that they were headed towards the market and thought they might be meeting up with Lillian. "I don't really have a misery plan, kinda playing it by ear actually."

"You have a lot of opportunity to move on. Maybe you should spend a little less time drinking at home and more in the pubs. We should try to go out more often, maybe with Lil and her friends." Connor opened the door to the market for James and continued. "Just because she is dead doesn't mean that you shouldn't have moved on years ago. She was brutal."

James kept his head facing forward so that Connor couldn't read his anger. "So where are we going? I don't think I heard you the first time."

Connor shook his head and told him that they were headed to the Market Grill. "Lillian is going to meet us", he added. James knew there was more to this than he was letting on; Connor was like that.

As they walked and James could feel his anger subside, he thought about Marie and what Connor meant by her being brutal. He just as easily recalled how easy it was to forgive her.

Drunk, absent minded, and lovingly he tried to focus on her face as he muttered, "I know you have been with other men."

She started to reply "of course…" but he put his fingers over mouth and told her to "shhhhhh".

She smiled as he continued, "I know that you have cheated on me. I don't care though because I know you won't again. I know the day you fell in love with me everything changed." He watched her facial expression change and he wasn't shocked. "I don't know who you have been with since me but I know that you haven't been with anyone since last Christmas. That's okay you know. You are still with me, and you are still with me for a reason."

Marie's smile faded and she played with James' hair with the hope that he would fall asleep. When she thought that his consciousness had faded she cried; he laid there with his eyes shut listening as her tears hit her pillow.

When they reached the restaurant and before Connor could go to the door James stopped him and looked seriously into his eyes, "I don't want you to talk about Marie like that anymore. I won't be able to hang out if you do and that would be sad to lose you too." Connor smiled and casually said "no problem", which caused James to be even more uneasy. They entered the building and Connor looked around and when he didn't see who he was looking for he asked for a table for four. "Who is the fourth?" James asked with suspicion of foul play. "You'll see" was the culprit's only response.

When they were seated Connor ordered two beers without asking what his company preferred. Within minutes Lillian came busting in through the door; that was the only way she ever really went through doors. She didn't even search the room before walking straight over to the table. Connor got up to give his wife a kiss and a smile. She leaned over to kiss James on his left cheek. "How's it going?" she asked generally as she took off her red jacket.

"Who else is joining us?" James asked knowing that she would tell him.

Lillian's eyes turned to her husband, "I thought you told me that he agreed."

"He doesn't know enough to agree yet so I made the executive decision." Connor responded defensively before taking half his beer down.

Lillian shook her head and admitted to James, "I never would have arranged this if he hadn't lied to me. This is a disaster." James looked towards the door as it opened and Lillian turned knowing that her friend was walking in to meet them.

The woman entered and James recognized the long arrow straight red hair, fair freckled face and voluptuous body. She approached the table wearing very tight and revealing clothing, though no one in the place was complaining about the inappropriateness of her attire. She stood beside the table awaiting a warm welcome and no one said a word. After a moment of awkward uncomfortable silence Connor stood and hugged her and then turned to James to say, "you remember Rachel." They both nodded in each other's direction, she smiled and sat knowing that there was something wrong.

Lillian excused herself and her husband from the table. "I just need to address a few things" she said with a smile before she dragged him into the woman's washroom to get him alone. James and Rachel were left with no one to talk to but each other.

As she let out, "how have you been", he muttered, "are you still working at. . . ." They both stopped to let the other finish; neither finished. Rachel looked around the room desperately searching for something to fix her attention on while James sought for a way to excuse himself. Nothing reasonable came to mind so he settled for the truth, "I am in love with a dead woman" he blurted out in desperation. Rachel's heart sank in disappointment. He continued, "I am going to leave now but it has nothing to do with you. I just need to be unhappy right now. It is a compliment to know that you are or were interested in me, thanks."

James got up and shuffled out of the booth, Rachel grabbed his arm and said, "when you are ready, can I be the one you call?" He nodded and smiled appreciatively. She released her grip so that he could run before the scheming couple returned; he did just that.

James had just stepped on the curb on the opposite side of the street before he heard Lillian's voice calling to him. Because it was Lillian he turned and yelled "what?" She held her finger up as if to indicate that he should wait and so he did. There was a clearing between the passing cars so she ran to him, the whole time looking straight into his eyes. She approached him and placed her two hands on his arms, "I'm sorry James". He looked at her and asked, "were you really in the dark?" She held tightly onto his arms and broke eye contact. She began, "he didn't tell me a thing, but I knew that he was plotting. When he told me that you had agreed to a double date with Rachel I knew there was no way he was telling the truth."

He quickly added, "then how could you?"

"I know you aren't ready now but I thought it would be a good idea to remind you that there is life out there for when you are ready. We all loved Marie, but she is gone and we can't just sit here watching your life fall away with her. It is for you James. She would do the same thing for me or Connor if one of us lost the other." Lillian let go of his arms and held hers open as a request for forgiveness; James hugged her loosely still not accepting that they expected him to move on.

"Tell Rachel I'm sorry" he said.

"I will" Lillian answered.

"Tell Connor he owes me a pack of cigarettes and a bottle of whiskey".

"I will", Lillian replied laughing with relief.

James walked away knowing full well that Lillian was watching him depart so with one hand he pulled his pants casually down to reveal one bum cheek. Lillian chuckled and took the hint; she headed back to what she could only expect to be a very awkward lunch.

He walked away mad at Connor. He couldn't blame him though because he didn't know the whole story. James made it back to his apartment and looked around remembering the last time he saw her alive.

Marie laid in her bed with her hands behind her head as she stared at her white plastered ceiling. She turned her head to her right and admired her handsome beau who lay innocently sleeping and unaware of what the day would bring.

She rolled over so her body was facing him and she pushed her fingers through his freshly cut hair. She smiled calmly and kissed him on the forehead before she rolled out of bed quietly as not to disturb him.

She could feel her weakness overshadowing her good mood but she put it out of her mind as fast as the thought had entered. As she made her way into the bathroom she caught a glimpse of herself and stopped dead in front of the mirror. She smiled to see a nicer reflection but even her bright white teeth couldn't hide her sunken eyes and her bloodless complexion. She let her hair down around her face and tried to play with it to make her look a little healthier; as she played with it she noticed how thin it was getting and she shook the hairs that had fallen out into the garbage. She stared straight into the glass and tipped her head to the right and told herself, "you are going to be beautiful today".

His muffled voice came from the bedroom, "what did you say?"

"Nothing honey" she chimed back with a hint of melody in her words.

Marie could hear the sound of a bed-headed man coming her way; he was making his usual morning growls and grunts. He came into the light of the bathroom and squinted his eyes with discontent. James curled his arms around Marie's waste, rested his head on her left shoulder and pretended to sleep. She smiled. He lifted his head once his eyes adjusted to the light and looked at her face in the mirror, "What are you doing there with your pretty little face?"

Smirking at his inability to fully open his eyes, "I am putting make up on, what does it look like?" she answered him.

"And why would you do such a thing today? You never wear make up around the apartment."

Avoiding eye contact, Marie answered him, "I think I am going to go out today, run some errands, get some air. I think I will put on that white dress that you bought me last year to celebrate the coming of spring and the departing of the snow."

"Well you better get ready quickly," he replied, "so that I can see how beautiful you look before I go to work."

He spun her around gently as not to hurt her and he kissed her on the forehead. She pulled away and contested, "I want a real kiss please." James felt a wave of guilt come over him as he realized that he had replaced passion with affection and he had long abandoned the lips for the forehead.

He pulled her in close to him and looked deeply into her eyes, "I really couldn't love you more than I do". He lowered his head to hers and kissed her with open lips on her mouth; he held her there for a minute before releasing her from the moment. After the kiss they looked at each other, smiled as if in appreciation and then simultaneously turned away to ready themselves for the day.

In the bedroom James heard Marie say something from the washroom but he couldn't make it out, "what did you say?" he called out.

"Can you go in late today so we can have breakfast?" she chimed back.

He stuck his second leg into his pants and walked over to her as he zipped them up. "Why would you ask me that? You know what I am going to say about being late for work and since when do you eat breakfast? Unless you were referring to a handful of pills and a glass of water as breakfast." He leaned against the door frame and watched Marie's reflection apply mascara. "Seriously though, what's up with you?"

She made eye contact with him through the antique framed mirror and smiled genuinely, "nothing's up with me, I just thought....I don't know what I thought. Forget I said anything at all." She neatly piled her makeup back into its case and turned to James for judgment, "how do I look?"

"Beautiful, like always." James looked as his watch, "I have to get going, I will bring you home some soup from work for you to eat tonight. Don't forget to check in with me during the day and let me know what you're doing and don't wear yourself out too much." He leaned in and kissed her forehead goodbye but quickly corrected himself and kissed her properly on the lips, "I love you baby".

"Love you too workhorse" she replied playfully. James walked away with a smirk, threw on a sweater and his shoes and head out the door. He walked to a job he hated and away from her forever.

Freeman sat anxiously in his doctor's office awaiting test results that he expected were flawless. When his physician of thirty years entered the room with chart in hand and a grim look his expectations were lowered slightly. Before the white coat could take his seat the impatient patient asked "what is it?"

His doctor cut the pleasantries and spoke honestly, "you have cancer, it is in your glands."

Freeman quickly rebutted with assertion, "So we can do treatment. Let's get rid of it" Freeman stated with assertion.

The doctor shook his head and said nothing, which spoke endlessly to the man who thought he was impenetrable.

After a short discussion about the disease and its implications, what he should expect and where they would go from now, the doctor asked Freeman about his kids and if he wanted help telling them. He answered, "I don't need to waste their time with this....I will tell them when it's over with."

The doctor looked at him with disbelief and replied, "Freeman, when this is over, you will be dead."

Freeman peered arrogantly back into the doctor's eyes and affirmed "when this is all over I will thank you for your opinion. I am a stronger man than you and it will take more than this to bring me down." He left the office with his physician following him asserting that he should be more realistic and start to prepare; he left the office with his chest out.

When he got to his sedan he got in to the driver's seat, put the keys into the ignition and turned the car on. He put both hands on the steering wheel and placed his head between them, taking a deep breath, reflecting on the news. He reached into his pocket and searched for it; he pulled out his cell phone, dialed and paused before pressing send. When he gained the courage he held the phone to his ear as it rang. It rang; it rang; Matthew's voice said hello. Freeman said nothing.

"Dad?" asked his son.

Freeman took a moment before perking up his voice and saying, "Hey Matt! How's it going? Just wanted to call to check in on you and the family."

"Good, good, how are you doing?" Matthew responded curiously.

"I am doing....hold on....look Matty, I am in heavy traffic here I better go....call you later okay?"

"Yeah dad, talk to you later."

Freeman hung up the phone. He placed the cell carefully back into his pocket and put the car's transmission into drive. He finished his day, like he had finished many days before, as if none of it had ever happened.

As Lillian approached the park down by the river where Samson had asked her to meet him, she couldn't help but wonder why he had requested her presence there that day. Not only was it frigidly cold but the pubs were so comfortably warm; the scenic venue had her guessing. She hopped down the path that lead to the bench where Samson sat seemingly at ease despite the arctic breezes. He recognized her hop and turned his head to verify what he already knew to be true.

"You made it" he stated, knowing that she wouldn't have let him down.

"I sure did." She answered. "Must say I am intrigued though, it's not every day that you and I hang out without Connor or, well, Marie."

"True enough" he said with a half smile.

"Shall we walk and talk to keep the blood flowing?" She asked as she exaggerated a full body shiver.

Samson nodded and rose from his comfortable position on the frozen bench. He offered her his arm and she ever so flirtily accepted it with her faux prissiness that everyone enjoyed; Samson smiled at the priss. They walked a mere five steps before she had to ask, "so what's up?"

"I need to talk", he answered.

"Obviously", she responded, "but what about? Or should I say who about?"

"Yeah, well, I think you've got me pegged."

"I thought as much. You miss her a little?" Lillian asked casually as if his girlfriend had gone on a week's vacation and she was teasing him about missing her. Samson picked up the pace a little and answered, "a lot".

The two unlinked their arms and walked for a minute or so without a word being uttered. Samson was the one to break the silence because he was the one with something to say, "I loved her Lil. I loved her so much. I don't think she knew how much, I don't even know if I knew how much I loved her."

Lillian took less than a second to declare, "she knew. She knew how you felt."

Samson stopped in his tracks and Lillian followed suit. "Then why did she pretend that she didn't? I mean, I told her once, but she played it off to be something else, something else, you know?"

Lillian took some extra time with this one to sort out the right, non offensive words, appropriate to such a delicate situation; she came up with something else. "Are you kidding yourself? I mean or are you kidding me? No....you are kidding yourself. She didn't for a second pretend not to know how you felt." Lillian took the palm of her hand and bounced it off of Samson's forehead. "Seriously though, are you this clueless or are you in denial to make this easier on yourself?"

Samson was taken off guard and was trying to figure out where the conversation just went; when he caught up he replied, "she never told me..."

"Of course she didn't. She respected you. She adored you. She loved you. Marie kept you at arm's length because she didn't want to hurt you and, more importantly, she didn't want to lose you."

The two started their momentum up again and their arms reconnected. Samson reflected on what Lillian just told him and she awaited his reaction. She didn't wait long. "Did she ever tell you these things or are these just things that you believe?"

"What do you think?"

"She said that?"

"She did", Lillian replied with confidence that she was doing the right thing. She decided that betraying the dead to heal the living wouldn't be an issue of negative karma.

The two walked, Samson's tears fell to the ground with little recognition, and when they came to a fork in the road the pair decided not to decide and instead sat on a nearby bench that was covered with a sheet of ice.

They made jokes about sliding right off and Lillian accidentally did as she joked, Samson laughed hysterically and almost forgot to help her up. When he helped her up she took advantage of the mood and reminded him of the time that Marie and Lillian had gotten him so drunk on tequila that they convinced him to pose in just a thong and a feathered boa for some questionable photos.

He laughed and reminded her, "and Marie blew them up and framed them all around my apartment that day I was bringing a girl back to have some sexy time. The two of you had the weirdest sense of humor." As the laughing subsided, the two regained their calm and resorted back to their former business faced selves. Lillian took a leap and asked what she always wanted to know, "did it kill you?"

Samson looked her squarely wondering, "which thing?"

"Seeing her with James…did it kill you?"

"It's funny you know; I loved nothing more than to see her happy. It was just too bad to see him make her happy."

"Was that an answer?"

"It was", he replied as he focused on the strange geese that never flew south for the winter, there was a family there. He watched what he assumed to be the mother goose, prune her young who, by the way, seemed less than impressed not to be in Florida. He continued, "it was all part of it. It was all part of being her friend."

"It was for you anyways."

"It was never easy for anyone to love her…in fact I bet the closer someone was to her the harder it would be."

Lillian chuckled and remembered something that one of the boys had said, "I feel sorry for any man who falls in love with Marie. They are destined to spend the rest of their life wanting something that no one will ever have." She paused, before admitting, "Jones told me that years ago, after Marie had gone home with her current fling. It always stuck with me because I didn't really believe that anyone could have such an effect."

"Were you wrong?"

"I wasn't right."

There was a pensive pause held by them both, "next time we'll talk about your feelings." Samson said feeling guilty about his need to be the centre of the conversation in this cold weather.

"No need. I am pretty sure that one of my roles in this life is to take care of the collateral damage from her leaving us. I am pretty good at it, and I don't so much mind the task at all", she admitted with little humor.

The two sat shivering silently on the bench before Connor called Lillian on her cell and requested their presence in a warm pub up the river; this was an offer that neither of them could refuse. The two had a good bonding hug when they stood and then raced up the icy hill towards the fireplace that awaited them.

Samson felt as if a weight had been lifted and Lillian felt as if she had done another good deed for her friend. Neither really cared about what really went on in Marie's head but, rather, relied comfortably on the ideal of the love of the deceased. The dead rarely deny false love, nor do they often admit love lost or any other sort of love for that matter.

Kay had tea steeping awaiting the arrival of her young friend. The elderly woman knew that the girl was coming from a funeral so she decided to be a lot easier on her today. She hadn't heard all the details but the girl's mother had called to offer the warning. When she arrived the girl came in like she always had with her sad smile though Kay did take notice that her eyes were dry with no sign of previous leaking. Kay offered a seat and set the tea down in front of her. The girl was suspicious; her older companion hadn't made one inquiry into her day nor had she made any comments on the black dress that she was wearing.

"Mom called you then" she muttered knowing the answer.

Kay hesitated, "she did call, do you want to talk about it?"

"Not really" the youth replied .

The elder sat down across from her and stared in silence; she knew that the girl couldn't bare the void in sound. So the girl began, "I didn't really like him anyhow. You don't have to treat me like a baby just because someone died."

"I am not treating you like a baby I just want to know what you are thinking. I always indulge you when you ask me questions, it can be your turn today" Kay answered.

Knowing that the wrinkled woman across from her was right, she thought for a moment before beginning. "Have you ever heard that someone died and you didn't feel sad about it but just weird?"

"I don't know what you mean. How do you feel weird?"she asked.

"I guess....I don't know....I don't feel anything about him or his life. I don't feel an absence really, or sadness, or anything at all. I don't feel guilty that I don't care nor do I feel bad for his family or anything."

"Your mother told me that you were very close to him when you were young."

"I guess you could say that" the girl answered irritably.

"So don't your fun memories make you miss him a little?" Kay questioned trying to get her to talk.

With frustration at the old woman's prying the girl let out "To tell the truth, I have been wishing him dead for many years." Kay's heart sank and the girl continued with her eyes fixed strongly on the linoleum floor. "He was a bad man who did bad things and he should have died a very long time ago. I think I may be a little sad about his death, but only because he didn't suffer like he deserved to. You can look at me however you want to", she said without moving her eyes from the ground, "and you can think I am terrible like my mother does but I know more than you think I do."

Kay said nothing as the girl paused; she didn't want to break the young woman's momentum.

The girl continued because she couldn't stand the silence and because she very rarely had someone listening to her so intently. "I realized today, as I sat in the funeral home listening to all these people saying wonderful things about him, that it doesn't matter when you are dead. It doesn't matter all the wonderful things you did or who you smiled to at work even though you had a bad day. What matters are the bad things you have done. Your life can't be measured by all the good things that are advertised for everyone to appreciate; it is the secret evil things that you have done in your life, the things that people don't want to talk about, that makes you. I sat there today looking around wondering how many other people were there that knew his evil deeds, who were affected by him. I never hated him for what he did, that would have created a bond between us, instead, I felt nothing.

I always thought that I wouldn't be me if it weren't for him; I wouldn't be untrusting, cynical, and intuitive. Maybe I would be those things but it is comforting to think that there was some reason for the things that he did, the shaping of my moral fiber is the reason I have assigned. He is dead now though and I am left with me and my memory. I wish I could erase my memory sometimes. I wish I could erase him so that I couldn't remember him ever being in my life." Her eyes were welling but she held strong and didn't let one tear escape.

Kay knew that it was her turn and she reached out to touch the girl's face but the younger pulled away and simply said "no touching". Kay listened to her and pulled back her hand.

The elder started, "Life would be much easier if we could just forget the things that hurt us. Life wouldn't be life though if we could. It is these memories of pain that teach us strength for the future. People who are never hurt may live happily but when the day comes, and it always does, that someone hurts them they will suffer more intensely because they have no scar tissue on their heart to protect them. He has shaped you; though I am sorry for how he did it. You are stronger for it and someday you will recognize this in yourself. Can I ask you a question, have you ever told anyone what he did to you?"

The girl, still looking at the floor in embarrassment for telling her secret so easily, didn't need time to think of an answer, "no I never told anyone. I was afraid they would think I was lying or worse they might think that I was doing it for attention."

"You are a lot stronger than I thought you were. Thank you for trusting me."

"Thank you for listening and believing" the girl replied with a forced half smile. "I should go" she said as she rose from her place. Kay didn't get up, she just let her leave without any fuss, the way she would want it. As she heard the heavy front door close Kay thought to herself that she never imagined that the girl would ever have any life experience or advice to offer, she then shook her head disappointedly at her own ignorance. She was sad though, knowing that this was the first time that the girl was able to open up and that it would most likely also be the last.

Tomas walked around the void that his brother called a home. The only things he had in the rental unit were scraps of metal and tools to mold them with. He was curious, "where do you sleep", he yelled towards the kitchen where Jones was at the moment.

He heard the reply, "wherever I pass out…you want a drink?" Tomas nodded, not considering that Jones couldn't see him, and his older brother entered the room with some random mixed drink in his hand. The younger took the muddy alcohol from his brother and took a sip without asking what it was; he didn't really want to know.

"What's this?" Tomas asked pointing at the large piece of what he assumed was supposed to be art laying against the wall.

"That's the sun. You see how I used those old springs to represent fire?" Jones asked.

"Nah" Tomas replied, "I don't get art. But I am sure that if I did I would appreciate this one."

"Yeah, guess I forgot who I was talking to there."

"Yeah", Tomas agreed with the insinuation that he was ignorant.

The two men sat on the hard wood floor and rested their backs against the wall; they sat about two feet apart and didn't say much but their train of thought was identical. Jones chuckled and Tomas, nervous but curious, asked what was on his mind.

"I was just remembering that summer when I moved back home before I went out West. I think you were like seventeen and Marie was nineteen, yeah, it was right before she went away to university."

Tomas knew what was coming, so he said nothing to urge the story along; Jones didn't need any persuasion to continue. "Remember you two got into a fight one day in the yard, I can't remember what you guys were fighting about, do you remember?"

"Nope, not sure when you are talking about exactly" Tomas added knowing very well where this was headed.

"Well anyhow, she was doing a painting outside…oh yeah…you went by and sprayed her with grass with the lawn mower and it stuck in the paint, that's why the two of you had it out. Do you remember?"

"Vaguely" he responded staring at the ground.

"Well, I remember that she owned you. Marie tore a strip off of you like only she could do; I was sitting on the porch and listening to her scream. So you, having the worst temper of any of us, took her canvas off the easel and threw it on the ground and then you ran the lawn mower over it. Do you remember, the mower stalled midway through tearing her painting to shreds?"

Tomas shook his head, "I think you might have dreamt this bro, I don't recall these events."

Jones took a sip from his drink, which he had made much stronger than his little brother's. He felt a wave of rage flow through his chest, "you should remember what happened next. Marie dropped to her knees and cried hysterically as she tugged her painting from underneath the lawn mower. After a few minutes she calmed herself and looked up towards you and said something. I couldn't make out what it was but it must have been pretty bad because you went over to her and punched her in the face. She bled everywhere, all over herself, I couldn't tell the difference between the blood and the paint all over her white shirt and her hands. I had planned on kicking your ass after I cleaned her up but as I wiped her clean she told me not to do anything to you."

"She never said that, why would she say that?" Tomas asked with disbelief.

"I thought that maybe you could tell me. Why did you hit her? What the hell were you thinking?"

"She pissed me off." Tomas asserted.

"But you punched a girl, on the ground crying, in the face. That's fucked. What did she say to you?"

"I don't remember."

Jones punched his brother playfully in the arm to counter the aggression that he was showing in his voice. "You sure you forget?"

"Let's just say that she said what she did so that I would hit her."

"It's funny that you say that Tom because that's exactly what she told me that day as I wiped the blood from her mouth. I thought she just told me that so that I wouldn't hurt you. But why would she want a punch in the face?"

"Jones, are you serious? Come on man. Are you really that oblivious to her manipulative ways? She wanted me to punch her so that I would have to live with what I did. I had to live with the guilt; my friends found out and wouldn't hang out with me; that chick Julie I was dating broke up with me when she saw Marie's face. She fucked me man." Tomas concluded his rant and bounced his head off the wall behind him.

"So basically she controlled her temper and channeled it in a short period of time to consider the worst punishment for your wrongs and she successfully manipulated you into doing exactly what she wanted you to do. Is that what you are saying here?"

"Yep. That is what I am saying here. She had mental problems... diagnosed mental problems. Why is it so hard to believe that a crazy person did something crazy?"

Jones shook his head, not really accepting what he just heard and finished his drink. The curiosity was killing him, "what did she say to you?"

Tomas took a second before he shook his head while saying, "sorry J, I will never tell. It died with her and I will take it to my grave."

Jones didn't reply but made a mental note to get Connor to join his mission to find out what was said that fateful day. After the two had finished their drinks Tomas stood up and said, "better go now". Jones stood up beside him and took the empty glass from his hand.

"Cool, thanks for stopping by little brother. You are welcome anytime; you should come over more often."

"You know that it might be more comfortable at mom's." Tomas offered.

"You know that isn't my scene anymore."

"Yeah Jones, not my scene either, but I live there so maybe you could stop by once and a while anyways."

Jones nodded his head ever so slightly in agreement and muttered, "I guess I could come by sometimes after she goes to bed, what is the average time these days?"

"About seven thirty" Tomas told him.

"Okay, will do."

The two towering men walked to the front door and gave a hug. Tomas opened the door and Jones stopped him to ask, "you know it's not cool to hit women right?"

Tomas laughed and said, "If I end up marrying a woman like Marie then I can't make any promises."

"Was that a really bad joke?" Jones asked hesitantly.

"Sure was" he replied "a really bad joke".

Tomas left and he decided to walk home; the entire two hour walk home he couldn't get Marie's words out of his head. The memory of her face calmly staring up at him and uttering to him; it was unshakable.

Jane pulled into Katherine's driveway as she heard her cell ringing in her purse. She quickly put the car in park and fumbled frantically through her bag attempting to answer the call. When she checked the call display she answered the phone with a bitter "hello". As she listened to Michael's questioning she looked up at the old house and considered driving away. "She called me to see if I wanted any of Marie's stuff" she answered "of course I don't but I need to see what she really wants." After a pause she continued, "She is probably lonely. It won't take long and I will be home before seven. Bye." Jane ended the call, opened the door and left the protection of her car. She looked up at the old elm tree that hovered over the driveway and shut her door.

Jane knew what to expect as she climbed the stairs that lead to the front door; she knew what to dread. As she stood on the porch waiting for Katherine to answer the door Jane looked down at the two chairs that faced one other. She smirked thinking about the times that they had sat there talking about nothing. She knocked a second time and the door opened slightly so she helped herself in.

The house was dark inside; the sun was lost there. She yelled out for Katherine and heard an ornery muffled response. Jane kicked her shoes off and walked through the messy kitchen and up the stairs towards the ramblings of an alcoholic; it had been quite some time since she had felt this nervous. She realized half way up the stairs that Katherine was in Marie's old room. When she came to the door she found the almost senior citizen sitting on the hardwood floor and haphazardly leaning against the bed. There were pictures scattered all over the place and Katherine was staring into space.

"Katherine?" Jane managed to let almost assertively out of her mouth.

Katherine turned her head to see who knew her name. "What are you doing here?" She asked aggressively before trying to drink out of an empty glass.

Jane replied with some hesitation, "You asked me to come"

"I don't want you here. Why would you come here? You don't have any reason to come here anymore." Katherine shut her eyes as if in deep meditation.

Jane walked around the bed and knelt just a bit more than an arm's length away from the drunken mourner. She looked at her lying on the ground and was sad that this once great matriarch had given herself to the bottle and had no intention of taking herself back.

She started to gather up the pictures, looking at the odd one. They were mostly of Marie and the boys when she was a little girl. One photo that Jane picked up made her stop to examine it for a moment. It was of Connor and Matt as little boys holding Marie (then under a year old) on Matt's lap. The baby girl was fussing and Matt had a very uncomfortable look on his face as well while, typically so, Connor watched his two unhappy siblings with an evil yet satisfied look on his face. Jane smiled until she looked up at their mother. "This is a funny picture" she said trying to rouse some interest or sobriety from her company; she received neither.

Jane observed this seemingly dead body before her and shook her head. She was familiar with this look in a parent. She had lost her father years earlier to this disease. Katherine's state reminded her of how life used to be; what had brought her and Marie to be so close.

"Are you a people pleaser?" Marie asked.
"Oh yeah", Jane responded.

"Is the approval of others more important to you than your own beliefs?"

Jane thought about this one and nodded.

"Do you have a drinking problem?"

Jane looked to the glass of wine that she was drinking and the two girls laughed at the same time. "I wouldn't call it a problem" Jane laughed.

"That's what all the alcoholics say", Marie laughed.

"I thought this was an 'are you the adult child of an alcoholic' test?"

"It is, now let me add up all our points and we will reveal the mystery", Marie diligently counted up the points and put her hands in the air as if she had won something, "I am the child of an alcoholic!" she said proudly. She looked back down at the sheet and then turned and pointed her finger towards Jane and said, "you my friend, are also the child of an alcoholic!" Jane put her glass in the air to cheers her friend in celebration.

"Well", Jane said, "It's good to get that out in the open."

"It sure is." Marie agreed.

The two sat back in their chairs and the smiles quickly left their faces as they heard a crash inside the house. Jane looked to her friend, "you want me to come in with you?"

"No thanks, you help me with her enough. Consider this your day off." Marie went inside and Jane sipped on her wine while listening to Katherine resist the help of her daughter.

When she had gathered all the pictures she put them neatly back into the box from where they came. She put the box back up into Marie's old closet. She took the blanket off of the bed and wrapped it around Katherine's shoulders as she snored. When she went downstairs she looked around the kitchen for the liquor. When she found it she dumped it; she felt quite satisfied with her actions.

She made her way back to the door and put her shoes back on but, before she left, she felt compelled to leave Katherine a message. She ran back into the kitchen and wrote her message down and then ran out of the house and back to her getaway car. She was ready to forget about it all over again.

Connor stumbled over a crack in the sidewalk. He realized at that moment that he might not be sober. He regained his posture and walked on. His hands were in the pockets of his nine year old tapered jeans. He noticed some young drunk girls passing him by and overheard a remark or two about his tie-dyed shirt. He smiled to himself and continued on his plight to find a pub that wasn't full of university students.

He walked by the Fox and the Pheasant and noticed that the bar was clear; he made his way down the stairs to the entrance. He shook the hand of the bouncer whom he had worked with years ago at the Hound Dog and the Hunter.

When Connor sat down at the bar he was feeling somewhere between sober and drunk. He needed to pass the threshold into numb; he still remembered everything.

The bartender approached him with a bottle of cold 50 in hand; Connor had been here before and the staff knew him well. "Thanks" said Connor. He took the beer in his hand and admired it appreciatively before he took a chug.

"No problem Connor" answered the bartender.

As he finished his first beer and before he received his second, Connor watched as the bartender was approached aggressively by a man dressed in a chef coat. He could only assume that the man arguing with the bartender and preventing him from getting his next drink was one of the kitchen staff.

He observed for a moment as the two abrasively addressed each other and didn't reconcile at all before the one in whites stormed away. Frustrated, the bartender approached the bar fly and asked, "can I get you another?"

"It isn't easy working with family" Connor asserted.

"No it isn't…how did you know?" asked the man behind the bar.

"I have a couple brothers that I have worked with before. It always ended up like you and yours."

"Wow…I didn't realize it was so obvious. We should watch that I guess."

"No, I think I just knew because I have lived it. Don't worry about it man, it happens when you are too close to your family." Connor said knowingly.

"You really seem to know what you're talking about. How many siblings do you have man?"

He sat for a moment, "I have three brothers and a sister."

"Where do you sit in the order?" the bartender inquired with false interest.

"I am the second oldest, but the first wisest."

The bartender laughed. "Well this round is on me for your familial insight." He handed Connor another bottle.

The poorly dressed man behind the bar focused his attention on the young women who had just entered the bar. Connor focused on his dripping beer; the condensation on the drink fondly reminded him of his sister's excessively sweaty hands. He laughed to himself. A few moments passed and he started to think of her psoriasis. He recalled a summer when she was scratching so hard her scalp was bleeding. In tears she asked him to make it better; he poured eighty dollar olive oil on her head. At the time he knew what he had to do but in retrospect he could have used canola.

Connor took his entire beer back and ordered another one with a side of whiskey. He still missed her. The bartender asked if he would like some peanuts to chew on. "No man, I am allergic to nuts" he answered sadly.

Connor took back the shot of whiskey and followed it with a half a beer. He remembered a time when Marie was eating M&M peanuts in his apartment. His throat started to constrict and she panicked and instantly threw the bag of chocolate covered nuts out the window. She begged forgiveness due to ignorance and then, feeling guilty, went outside to pick up the litter outside his window. From that day forward she never ate another peanut due to the empathy for her brother. He thought she was ridiculous then but understood her empathy better now.

Connor took back the rest of his beer and ordered another round. He tried to remember what he was thinking about, but could not. He sipped his beer and focused on remembering what he was thinking about, but failed again. He took his second shot of whiskey and paid attention to the girls on the other side of the bar. They weren't as interesting as the bartender made them seem.

As he finished his beer he noticed a vision entering the bar. She was beautiful and vibrant. She was better than all of this, he thought. She walked across the bar and spoke to him "Babe, you weren't that easy to find this time".

"Sorry" he replied. Lillian patiently waited for him to finish his drink and they headed out the door.

On the walk home Connor spoke very little. Lillian prodded him with a few questions to see what his mind was up to. He said few things but they were all about his sister; he told her about the peanuts out the window and about the olive oil. "I wouldn't believe those stories if I hadn't been there myself" she chuckled. Connor stopped dead when they reached their house and held Lillian by her shoulders, "I think I miss her."

"That's okay you know. It isn't bad to miss someone you love when they are gone."

Connor swayed back and forth, let out a deep burp and mumbled, "Just don't tell her Lil. That's not our way."

"I know babe. I know. Let's get to bed."

The couple entered their apartment and Connor passed out on the floor beside their bed. Lillian tried to wake him but gave up quickly. She got ready to sleep and lay in the middle of their double bed. She was happy for the first time since Marie's death, Connor was admitting to missing her. This just might lead to him forgiving her for leaving him.

James kicked a bobby pin under the couch and wondered how those god forsaken pins could still be laying around almost a year after she had disappeared. He decided not to drink today; this was a new day. The one year anniversary of her death was around the corner and he couldn't be a depressed lush when he visited her. He opted to do something he hadn't done since she left; he decided to clean their apartment. The place was so disastrous the only person who was unaffected by the mess, and would still visit, was Connor.

James began with the washroom, cleaning the toilet and sink, and moved through the living room tidying and throwing away old cigarette butts. He cleaned diligently, at no time entering the bedroom, saving the hardest task for last. When he dumped the mop water in the kitchen sink he admitted to himself that there was only one place left to go; he made his way into their bedroom.

He looked at the pile of her clothes in the corner and he said, "you were such a slob". The layer of dust on her clothes took flight when he picked them up and caused him to drop the load when he started sneezing uncontrollably. He picked up a piece from the pile that he recognized, it was what she wore their last night together. He could remember her laughing at him; she kept pulling up the black strapless dress by its top because she had lost so much weight and it was falling off of her bones.

He had pretended to be a sumo wrestler and, because she kept laughing, he kept up the charade until they got home and her laughter faded. He could feel the way he felt that night, so confused at her affection and coinciding distance. If only he had known what was to come, he would have said so much.

James shook his head and picked up the rest of her clothes. He decided between the laundry and the garbage; she would not be happy to know that her favorite dress was in the trash so he dumped the burden in his hamper.

James then turned to meet his demon. He approached the painting on the easel and placed his gripping hands on either side. He looked at it wondering whether or not it was finished and then, placed his forehead against the canvas and laughed. He realized that if the painting wasn't finished that she would still be here. He picked it up and took it into the living room where he found a random nail in the wall, he placed it there the way she always hung her paintings. James threw all Marie's painting supplies into a box and placed it into the closet for storage. He didn't cry nor think about crying.

It was time to clean himself; he showered and, for the first time in nearly a year, he sang the wrong words off tune to Lean on Me by Bill Withers. He turned the water off and reached out for a towel with which he did not dry himself but merely tied around his waist. He always loved a good drip dry on a cool spring day. He returned to the bedroom to check his email.

His mother had emailed him requesting some contact from him when he was ready, he deleted the message. It occurred to him that maybe he should clean out his email as well, and so he started opening old emails from Marie. There was one in particular that he recognized by the subject line 'could I love you more?' He opened the email with his heart breaking.

He smiled remembering how she came up behind him when he opened it the first time. He had read the message which said, *I owe it all to you, check out the dedication*, and she came up behind him and hugged him so hard with excitement that he started choking. "I haven't even read the dedication yet", James said to himself, getting caught up in the memory. He clicked on the attachment and the final copy of her book popped up.

Conversations with Kay read the title and, as he turned to page two, he read her dedication and was reminded of her logic. He smiled and held back a laugh because he was upset with the foresight she hid away for herself. He stared at the words on the screen until they made some sense to him, or knocked some sense into him.

James reached for his cell and searched for a number. He dialed, the phone rang, his palms sweat and a woman answered. He said nothing. "Hello" she answered again. He said nothing still.

"James?" She asked knowing that it was him by the number on the phone.

"Hi", he replied nervously, "Hi Rachel, I was wondering if you would let me take you out to apologize for being rude last month at the diner".

"Have you ever regretted any of your choices? Any of your major decisions?" The girl asked of Kay while sipping on her peppermint tea. She was asking because she was sure the answer was no and that was just what she needed to hear.

"No", replied the elderly lady, "I would never be dumb enough to make a choice that I would regret, plus it is just not in my nature to make bad decisions."

The youth chuckled at Kay's false confidence and unrealistic portrayal of life. "Do you really believe what you just said?" She asked with a smirk.

"Of course I believe it...there are, of course, decisions that I have thought about ever since I made them; But not, of course, because I have regretted them. There is no room in life for regret you know."

"I know", the girl replied, "that was one of my lessons remember?"

"Of course it was", her elder replied confidently. "You know what? There have been times that I have made a decision that I have wondered what my life would have been like had I made a different decision. No regrets of course, just a sense of 'what if'" Kay poured the girl some more tea and shuffled back to the stove before finding comfort in her heavily cushioned seat. "I guess that I may regret a decision that I made for someone else, but I don't count that really because it was one of those selfless acts....you know, something you do because it would benefit someone else more than yourself?"

"Yeah I know what a selfless act is." The girl replied resentfully. "What was yours Kay?"

The wrinkled woman smiled knowingly in her place and paused, honestly debating whether or not to continue this conversation. She opted to move forward for the sake of the young. "I loved someone once. I loved them very much but they never really knew where I stood."

The girl took a sip of her minty tea and questioned, "that doesn't sound like a selfless act, it sounds like you were too afraid to express yourself".

Kay shook her head, "he needed me; he needed someone to love him. He needed someone to care that he wouldn't lose, someone that would always be there for him. I loved him unconditionally because he was wonderful but, most of all, because he had no idea how wonderful he was. And, you smart ass, it was a selfless act because I wanted nothing more than to be with him, but I knew that I would do nothing less than hurt him. I stood aside, to his dismay and mine, helping him try to carve a life out of the world of negativity before him. At first it was torturous because he was so dark, lonely and desperate for more and I was all he had. It became harder for me though; ironically easier for him; when he fell in love. He had everything I always wanted for him but I remained the same; not bad, but effected. I gave a toast at his wedding and, until the day he died, he was my closest friend. I wanted nothing more for him then what he made for himself; nothing hurt me more though then to hear him tell me how much he loved this life that I helped him create." Kay closed her eyes as if holding back tears, but the girl couldn't be sure. The old woman before her didn't often seem so vulnerable. The youth couldn't think of much else to say so she settled with, "Did you ever tell him?"

"Tell him what?" Kay quickly asked.

"Did you ever tell him how you felt?" She answered.

"I didn't tell him. I couldn't do that to him. There is a piece of me, maybe it is egocentric or unexplainable hope, but I honestly think that he would have let it all go for me. I think that he might have walked away from happiness to be with a fraction of me: all that I could give him. When he looked at me I could see how he felt in his eyes, in his smile. If I said the word he might have left everything good to spend his life with a shell of a person, with someone who couldn't give him everything."

"How did you two stay friends after all those years?" The youth asked genuinely interested in this intriguing information.

"I was a good friend to him, as he was to me; love is the greatest basis for an excellent friendship I have found."

The girl nodded her head as if she had had a taste of such things. Her mind struggled to comprehend these ramblings of the elderly lady; it was always difficult for her to imagine Kay as a young woman. Ideas popped into her head though, "What about your husband? Did he know that you were in love with another man? I thought you were madly in love with him?"

Kay paused, looked to the bottom of her teacup, and was overcome with anger. She got out of her seat aggressively and made her way over to the sink. She opened the lower cupboard where most people would keep their garbage and cleaning products and pulled out a bottle of Dubonnet. She poured herself a glass, hesitated, and then poured a glass for her younger counterpart. The girl was shocked at the alcohol and more so at the offering. Kay began, "Have you ever been in love little girl? I ask only because I know that you think you have been. Am I right?"

"Yes" she replied hesitantly.

"Well, I know you haven't by the questions that you ask me."

"What questi..."the girl began.

"Never mind that now", Kay cut her off, not wanting to waste her words. "I could never love anyone more than I loved my husband, that is why HE was my husband. This man I am talking about I knew for many years before I settled down. He was a friend from my youth, a person that I always respected and admired. I always loved him but knew that I would only hurt him because of the way that I was. My husband, when I met him, made me want to be a better person; he made me want to be good; he made me realize that I could be good. The difference between them is that the first I loved because I wanted to help him be as wonderful as I knew he could be, the second I loved because he helped me be as wonderful as he knew I could be." Kay stopped, and spun her rouge beverage around in her glass thinking about her husband's smile. She smiled.

"Would you change anything now if you could?" The girl asked, curious of what the reply may be.

Kay swirled her Dubonnet, staring into the abyss of the eddy. She thought about her answer before giving it, a rarity the girl thought to herself. Kay finally responded, "Though it hurts me to think about the men in my life and how I reacted to them, I wouldn't change a thing. I wouldn't be me if I had taken any other route. I am not one to follow the yellow brick road, though dancing across it is satisfying. I just chose to dance with one man in particular while casually glancing at another who danced with his love; this is the way that dancing works."

"Your metaphors are ridiculous and they rarely make sense", the girl asserted.

Kay said finally because she felt she had to. "That's only because you lack the imagination to comprehend anything beyond your short and simple life. Because you are jealous of experience and hate when you can't pretend to relate to something I say. Because you can't accept that I am sixty years older than you and that I might have more experience than you in life."

"That isn't true," the girl argued.

Kay felt a little guilty for coming down on the girl. The elder was just angry because she awakened many emotions by talking about her past that she had long suppressed. "I'm sorry", she replied regretfully.

A young girl, so eager to be apologized to by this respected elder, accepted the token immediately. The two sipped on their fortified wine, the younger choking it down and the elder wondering why she ever gave up drinking. The girl believed that this was the end of a very awkward and unproductive conversation; Kay hadn't felt this satisfied from a talk for years.

Chris cut through central park as he had fought through traffic more effectively today than usual. He realized that fall had arrived by the changing colors of the leaves. He barely noticed the coming and passing of summer from his office on the thirtieth floor.

It was nice to feel the breeze of autumn on his face this day. He, getting caught up in the moment, sat down on a park bench. He watched the people pass him by; comforting to be the one sitting still. He watched a new mother coach her screaming child as they walked by. He laughed at a couple arguing as they passed him, the woman walking five feet in front of the man with him looking very nervous and confused about her anger.

He smiled watching a young woman in a suit whose heel had snapped in the interlocked brick. She didn't get mad; she laughed out loud, took both shoes off and walked barefoot. This woman reminded him of someone; he couldn't put his finger on it. As she was in the distance she threw her shoes in the garbage; Chris thought that was an odd move as she wouldn't have proof of her mishap. It wasn't a smart move he thought to himself, she wasn't thinking clearly.

Chris glanced at his watch and got up off the bench. As he took his first step he realized that it was Marie that the shoeless woman reminded him of. She was clumsy, had a good sense of humor and would walk barefoot in a public area; just like Marie. He sat back down on his bench. His smile turned to a frown. The thought of her hadn't crossed his mind in months. Guilt surfaced heavily to his chest; he hadn't felt this bad in fifteen years.

Chris frantically pulled on his jacket as he ran for the ringing phone; he was late for an important meeting. "Hello?" he answered in a hurry.

"Chris? It's Katherine", the voice said on the other line.

Chris said nothing in shock of this call. He came to his senses and replied, "yeah, it's me. What?...I wasn't expecting to hear from you Kate."

"I am sorry to call you like this, but Marie wanted to talk to you. She keeps asking about you and I don't know what to tell her", Katherine replied.

This is against the agreement that you laid out for us. What are you doing?" Chris was confused and emotional.

A little voice came on the line, "hello?"

Chris said nothing and tears flowed from his eyes. He tried to clear his throat casually, "Marie?" he asked. He brought his fist to his mouth and he couldn't keep from crying.

"Hi Chris!" The eleven year old's voice chimed happily on the other end of the line. "Where are you? Why don't you send me back your next move?" The young girl was asking of their chess game they were mailing back and forth.

"I am sorry Marie, we might not be able to play anymore." He explained guiltily.

"But why? I was going to beat you is that why?" The child asked him honestly.

Chris stopped not fully knowing what answer he would give her. He settled with, "yes, you are too good and I hate to lose Marie. Maybe you should play a game with Tomas or your mom."

"But I like to play with you" she replied, "you are the reason I like to play, and I even joined the chess club at school."

"We'll see", he told her, "can I talk to mommy please?"

"Okay", she consented, "will you come and visit us again soon?" she asked with hope in her voice.

"Next time I am in that area I will visit you", he promised deceitfully.

"Okay, here's mom" she told him.

There was a noise of the phone being passed on clumsily. "Chris?" Katherine asked wondering if he had hung up.

"I am here", he replied unimpressed. "Why do you do this to me?" he asked with tears in his eyes.

Katherine was silent for a few moments. "She kept asking about you. I didn't know what to tell her. She misses you."

"Why would she miss me?" Chris asked broken hearted.

"I don't know", Katherine replied, "but she won't leave it alone."

"This was your deal Kate." Chris said coldly, "You need to sort this out on your own."

Katherine fought back the tears and replied, "I know. I am sorry I called."

"This is impossible for me do you realize that?" Chris admitted.

Katherine didn't realize it, though she said, "I do, I'm sorry." She didn't know what else to say so she asked, "how is your mom?"

"Dead", he responded coldly.

There was silence and then, "I am so sorry," Katherine said in shock.

Chris remembered his hurry, "I need to get going" he told her.

"Bye Chris" She said.

He hung up his phone and thought about Marie's little voice asking him to play with her. He went into to his filing cabinet at home and took out her file. He spread it out in front of him. All the pictures that Katherine had sent him over the years to taunt him were present; his correspondences with Marie playing chess; the letter from the clinic with the wrong name on it; a tape of Lionel Ritchie singing Ballerina Girl; everything that ever reminded him of her. He picked up his phone and dialed work to call in sick.

It hadn't even been a year since she died and he had already forgotten her. He would never forget her. He loved her. She was the daughter he always wondered if he had. He laughed to himself; she would be so mad at him right now. He picked up his phone and called in sick for the second time in his life. He spent the day on that park bench watching people and talking to strangers.

Katherine woke up the morning after June had accosted her to attempt sobriety. She was not happy. She was not hung over for the first time in years; she was worse: sober and feeling everything. June greeted her with breakfast in bed and a smile. "Here you go, you will love this, my famous French toast."

"When are you leaving?" Katherine asked with irritation.

"When I have done what I came to do", June said honestly.

"What's that?" Katherine asked.

"I want to you to be sober and read the letter that your daughter wrote you before she died." June answered.

"How did you find that?"

"You gave it to me to read and you told me that you wished you could understand what she meant by it." June explained.

"I did not".

"You did. Last week. You handed me the letter and your cried as I read it because you couldn't understand what it meant." June set the meal down on her friend's legs and put the fork in her hand. "You need to be sober to understand this. Eat."

Katherine ate. She ate though she felt nauseous. She was unsure whether the nausea was a direct result of the sobriety or the being faced with Marie's madness. She ate because her lifelong friend watched her like a hawk as she chewed every bite. She wasn't accustomed to eating breakfast.

As Katherine suffered her food down, June thought to ask, "what would you like to do today? We could go for a walk, go to a museum, see a movie, anything you want", she offered in as positive a voice as she could muster.

Katherine leered at her friend and uttered, "let's get it over with then."

June nodded. "Just what I thought you would say. I will let you finish eating." As her friend choked down the eggs politely June reached into her bedside table and took out the hand written letter. *It was so simple* June thought to herself, *it was almost beautiful*. "Shall I read it to you". She asked.

"I can read it myself", Katherine said almost throwing the food aside to grab the letter. She took the paper from June's hand and read to herself.

Mom,

Remember,
Some things happen in life because they are meant to happen,
Some things happen because we make them happen.
You have decided to set yourself apart from others,
Not for greatness but for weakness.

Decide how you want to die because you are the only one who can.

Keep drinking and it will happen fast and it will be a lonely death.
Or die some other way, with people there to care that you are dying.
Trust me when I say that it is difficult to die alone.

All my sadness for you,

Marie

Katherine read it three times before she spoke aloud, "So." She looked at her friend expecting anger.

June calmly replied, "You should keep reading it until it means something to you."

"Nothing's going to change." Katherine responded.

"Then you really have decided to be alone?" June asked sadly.

"You can't listen to what she says here. She was cracked. She was unstable and didn't know what she was talking about. June, she killed herself. She wasn't in her right mind. Are you seriously reading this as if it means something?" Katherine was out of bed now and violently going through her drawers looking for clothes to wear.

June's face was solemn. "She said in that letter what she could never say to you in life. She died Katherine, and the very last thing she said to you was in that letter. Do you want to die alone like your daughter did?"

Katherine laughed, "I will never be alone. I will always have Tomas and you."

"You won't" June said with uncharacteristic assertiveness. "I am going to pay for Tomas to live in an apartment by himself; I can't let you ruin him too. You choose which life you want. We won't be here for you much longer."

"June, who are you kidding. You can't do that. I lost my daughter, I am just having some trouble dealing with it", Katherine said uneasy about June's new found confidence.

June took a deep breath and let out, "You have been broken for too many years and far longer than Marie has been dead. You are selfish, and you need to see what you have done to your children, all of them." June picked up the tray of half eaten food and walked to the door, "You are sober now and have been for over a day, make your choice." June left the room, washed the dishes in the kitchen and left the house without another word with her friend, though it killed her to do so.

Katherine watched from her bedroom window as her oldest friend abandoned her. She went back to her bed and lay down. She picked up the paper with the horrendous handwriting on it. She reread the words. She had never resented her daughter's advice in life but she hated it now. She crumpled up the page and threw it in the direction of the garbage. She yelled out, "Tomas! Tomas?!" There was no response.

She didn't know where he would be; Katherine realized that she didn't know anything about him now. She couldn't remember how his hair was cut or how he looked in his glasses. She couldn't recall any recent conversations with Tomas or any of the other boys.

Katherine thought back to the last time she was confronted by her children,

"You have a problem", Matt said to his belligerent mother, "you need to get help, you are killing yourself"

"I am fine." She assured her flock of children gathered together for the first time in months.

"You are hurting us too" Connor added to his brother's original statement.

Katherine laughed condescendingly, "you are fine....look at you all, you are more than I ever expected."

"You aren't understanding what we are trying to say, you are not just killing yourself but you are seriously fucking us up in the meantime", Marie said with a straight emotionless face.

"Wow, you are dramatic, this is ridiculous. Isn't your sister being dramatic?" She asked the boys as she leaned against a wall to support herself.

"You have a problem, you are addicted to this shit and you need to stop" said Jones.

"That is stupid.....you can't be addicted to alcohol." Your father told you to say that, he is turning you against me.

"Mom....please listen to us." Matthew pleaded, "If you care about me at all you might listen to what I am saying. You have a problem that requires help and we are here talking to you to help you and guide you to the next level."

"I don't have a problem. I am not stupid and I don't need your help. If you all feel like ganging up on me then do so, but at least make it for a valid reason like I have ruined your lives or something."

Marie, with invisible retracted tears said, "mom...you need to choose. You can be sober and be with us or you can drink and be alone. I know you don't want to lose us mom....I know you don't want to be alone."

Katherine leered at her daughter in anger and said with wrath, "I don't need you, any of you. I can't believe you are all making such a big deal out of nothing. This is ridiculous and I think that you all should leave.

"We didn't come here to leave", said Jones.

"I think you did" replied the drunken matriarch.

Jones replied, "I see. You want it that way do you?"

Katherine looked coldly away and said, "Good bye."

"I am sorry that you feel that way" Jones replied, "In that case, I will miss you.....the sober you. But thanks for the release, because I couldn't have done it without you. The problem is you mom, no one else, so please come to terms with that. And Please, if nothing else, realize how you have hurt us over the years." Jones picked up his jacket and walked out the old screen door, which dramatically slammed as he walked away in anger. The others remained in silence and fear.

Katherine ran to the door and almost fell through the screen as she screamed, "YOU ARE THE ONE WITH THE PROBLEM! IT ISN'T ME! YOU WILL BE BACK! YOU NEED ME!"

Katherine stood at the door; more alone than she has ever stood. She just forced her eldest son to walk away from her; he wouldn't be back.

She turned to the remaining four. "What about you Matt? You ever going to live up to your big fucking mouth? Are you ever going to do anything worth talking about?" Matthew's lip quivered and he remained silent because he didn't want to give her the satisfaction of tears. She turned to Connor and continued, "and wise Connor, why don't you go read a book about it and then declare yourself an expert. Do they write books on how to turn away from your family? Do they Connor?" Connor remained unshaken as he was expecting everything. "And Tomas, do you think I can't see you hiding behind your brother? You little fucking coward."

"Mom stop", Marie said nervously.

"Oh I'm sorry little princess, am I saying something offensive? Well you are one to talk when we all have to put up with your fits, you crazy bitch." Katherine stepped closer to her daughter and Marie braced herself, but she didn't touch her. Instead, the matriarch went up to her bed and passed out.

Though Jones was the first to leave on that day, the others were going to follow one by one, starting with Connor who would find reason in his brother's rational, then Matt. Marie would leave her by death, and now Tomas who would leave her for a hope of life beyond this.

    She remained laying on her bed. She wept. She wept for herself, for the choice she had to make. She had to choose between the family she had left and numbness; it didn't seem fair. *That is no choice at all* she thought to herself. Katherine went to the kitchen to make herself a drink and she couldn't find anything; June cleared it all. She stopped by the notepad on the counter and read: *now is the perfect time to change the rest of your life*. It wasn't in June's handwriting but it was clearly female, she couldn't figure out who wrote it but she also couldn't focus long enough to care.

    She wept passionately hoping that her tears would wash away the ultimatum of sobriety versus family; they did nothing but make her tired. And so she slept; she slept for days.

    When she woke she decided to die on her own terms.

James approached the door and took his keys out but, before he tried to unlock the door he paused. There was a time when he knew that she wouldn't lock the door as he had asked her to. He reached out and turned the knob; the door was locked now.

There was a time when he would have been angry to come home to an unlocked door; now he longed for that unjustified rage.

He would feel some sort of protective rage flow through him but he couldn't acknowledge it because he had accepted her flagrant ways years previous when she had explained them to him in detail. He entered whilst taking in a deep meditative breath to refresh his attitude.

"You here?" He yelled out knowing very well what the answer was.

"In the bedroom" she replied.

James removed his bag and his jacket making his way back to their room. He walked and knew she was writing because she hadn't met him with excitement at their door; her writing was the only thing that kept her from him lately. "Are you writing? Do you want me to leave and come back?" he offered knowing what her response would be as it was the same every night lately.

"It's okay", she said surprising him, "I am done for now". She finished typing her last few words of the day and she turned her chair towards him and smiled affectionately. "How was work?"

"Same as always. How was being a bum around the house?" He asked with a chuckle.

"Same as always." She said before realizing that it wasn't the same as always at all.

"Actually," She stalled, "maybe you can help me with something."

James layed down on the bed across from her desk and said, "shoot."

"I am having some trouble deciding what the real representation of Kay and the girl's relationship is. Like I don't know what they are a metaphor for."

"Why can't they just be an old woman and a young girl? I mean, that's what they are right?" James asked earnestly.

"But baby, that's not the way literature works. Something always represents something else, everyone knows that. These two characters are more than two people, I just haven't figured that out yet." Marie let out a frustrated sigh and spun around in her computer chair.

James smiled, humoring his love, "I think that authors know before they write a story what their characters are supposed to represent...I doubt it is an afterthought like it is with you."

Not even remotely attempting to hide her rage she let out aggressively, "the reader is supposed to wonder, like I wonder now. They won't know until the end what they represent just as I don't. That's the romantic relationship an Author has with his reader, they share a secret."

James smiled at her interpretation of authorship, "really? What exactly is that relationship?"

"Much like any relationship; two people are dancing back and forth trying to find a connection. Depending on degrees of desperation, it doesn't take much to find it. A person writes, or says something that the interpreter takes as an intimate connection that neither understand. It is a silent connection that binds them. "James", Marie said fondly, "that's why I love you. There is an unexplainable connection between us that will bind us forever despite the fact that neither of us understand it.... It is also why I hate biographies and other truthful tales; my heart and mind finds no bond with reality."

James smiled as he fell more in love with a woman he had already thought to be the ultimate example of greatness, weakness and hope. He was starting to be reminded of his lost unquestionable faith in a god.... she hadn't quite reached the territory of a diety yet...maybe in another life he thought. His frown surfaced but when he raised his head to face her for sympathy he saw the tears fall from her now porcelain like face. He reached out his right hand and held her chin, "What's wrong?" he asked.

"I need to finish this book James. This book is my everything."

James' heart broke hearing those words from her mouth; his heart broke because he knew that that damn book did mean more to her than anything. More so he knew that she was on a deadline, though he didn't know how soon that deadline was approaching. He held back his own tears and turned his hand to her powder like cheek bone to tell her, "There is nothing I want more for you than to see you finish this book. I think you might be getting a little stressed though, you have more time than you think." Marie sat silently before him and she wouldn't release any tears; a sign, he thought, that she may be leaving him sooner than he planned.

"How do you feel today?" he asked.

"Worse than yesterday but better than I will tomorrow, I need to finish my story," she said with hurtful frustration.

"Maybe you should try to take it easy. Relax a little, spend some more time with Lil and Connor"

"I am too tired for them," Marie said, "they will wonder what is wrong with me. Lil knows me too well, she will confront me and I will have to tell her the truth and I think that Connor suspects that I am pregnant."

James smiled and asked, "Is that because you have lead him down that path?"

"Connor is a smart guy, he makes the decisions of what he wants to see and what he doesn't" Marie said knowingly.

James thought about it and agreed, "true enough" he said.

Marie's hand casually pressed in on her stomach as she tried not to reveal her pain through her face but James noticed her discomfort, "you okay?" he asked concerned.

"I am fine," she insisted, "just feeling a little sick. Going to lay down for a minute."

James took her face in his hands and kissed her on the forehead and asked, "you need some more medication?"

"I am maxed out for today I think. I just need to rest". Marie laid down on the bed and he tucked the blankets in around her. He sat on the bed and caressed her hair until she fell asleep; she even winced in her sleep now. He glanced to the night table and observed that her medication had double in the past few months. There were just over ten prescription bottles, all different sizes and shapes. They sat there like the towering buildings in New York, making him feel insignificant. *It is funny*, he thought, *when life's comfort is dependent on medication that divides you from yourself.* James got up to turn the lights out when he noticed the computer was still on. He moved the mouse to reveal the last page that Marie had written; he scrolled down to the last line: *Kay thought of how she was left behind to remember all those she had loved; this girl was the only one left to remember her. This girl was everything.*

James sensed that Kay was going to die soon in this story.

He turned off the computer, stripped his clothes off and shut the lights. He was far from tired but he laid down beside his girl and he pulled her close, her head in his chest. She stirred but she was weak and her medication was strong, when she squeezed him, he could barely feel it. She slept in his arms and he cried quietly to himself as not to wake her. He wondered how many nights he had left to hold her; as long as it took her to finish the book he guessed.

James focused on the present as he poured himself a rum and soda. He needed to try and move on and, though he knew it would be difficult, he needed to let go of some of her. He knew where to start: the letter she sent him. He took his drink in hand and marched into the bedroom; he kept her hand written letter under her old pill bottles. He reached for it and read it as he drank:

James, my brilliant man,
There is something to be said about a person who has remained untouched by death or personal tragedy throughout their life. When you look into their eyes they are free from the lingering darkness that possesses others. Their hearts are open, unguarded and naïve but, more importantly, blissful. When I met you, I saw happiness in your eyes. I don't know whether I was envious of you then or perhaps just hopeful that you could share it, but now I know that your scar free heart was only that because you had not yet met me.

You loved me like no one could, for reasons that I will never understand. You wanted to know my pain, you tried to understand my mind; your frustration was unmistakable. Thank you for that.

Thank you also for keeping my secret. I know how we fought about it and I know that keeping it in was impossible for you but I expect that you will hold it inside of you until you can no longer. You are strong but you can't carry my weight forever. People will say things about me that will hurt, try not to let my secret out in order to protect me; you don't need to protect me anymore.

You don't owe me anything; please don't mourn yourself into a silly depression (you know how I feel about silly depressions). I will be with you as long as you want me to be and when you are ready to let go, I will too. Let someone someday enjoy the best of you as I have.

You are a fantastic man with endless potential, the most beautiful person I know. You mean so much to me; I wish that I could have been stronger for you. I wish that I could have been here longer for you.

Never forget the truth about us and how great we were.

Love,

me, a figment of your imagination.

James considered his options for facing this written reminder of his beloved Marie. He narrowed it down to burning the letter or just throwing it into the garbage. This was a big step to recovery he decided.

He put it back under the pill bottles for safe keeping while he deliberated over his options. James then curled up with her pillow and fell asleep contently.

"How did you know?" the girl asked as she swept Kay's porch.
"Know what?" asked Kay from her comfortable old chair.
"How did you know when you met the man for you?"
Kay smiled and leaned back into her chair as if in contemplation but, the truth be told, she knew what her response was from the second she heard the question. She forced the smile from her face in order to seem sincere and she answered the girl as honestly as she knew how.

"The thing is that any man you are with is the 'man for you'."

"That is not true Kay, there must be more to love than that." The girl stopped sweeping at this point and just leaned on the broom awaiting some sort of romantic explanation that she had already accepted wouldn't come.

"Well, if you are with someone, he is the man for you, right now. When he is no longer fulfilling whatever need you were keeping him around for, then he will no longer be your man because you will move on to someone else."

The girl was less than satisfied with this answer so she resumed her chore. "I don't think that you believe what you are saying" she voiced with distaste.

Kay missed her last comment because she was admiring a leaf deporting from its roots and gracefully sailing down to the ground. "Fall is here" she announced knowingly. "Fall is the season that most inspires me you know? The temperature is perfect and summer's is the only funeral that I look forward to. The sadness and beauty of this season is unparalleled." Kay sat back in her chair comfortably and shut her eyes in meditation which was very shortly disrupted.

"So I can guess that you are changing the subject because you don't want to give me your actual answer to my question. Why not just say so?" Girl asked.

Kay opened her eyes as her thought process had been compromised. "That was my answer; the first part of it at least. Just because you don't have the patience to let an old woman think, doesn't mean that I am trying to pull the wool over your eyes." Kay shook her head in fake frustration. "As I was saying…any man you are with can be the man for you. The reason why most marriages fail is because people settle for this: a person that they love, or think they love. If you can hold out, someday you MIGHT find the man that you are meant to procreate with. Love, my dear, is only one thing you need to have a good and lasting relationship. Basing your life on love and love alone will only lead to disaster; too much passion there. The key is to figure out for yourself what else matters."

After thinking for a minute the girl asked, "you mean like they should be funny, caring, patient?"

"Depends on what matters to you. Think of it like a business deal: you need to create a relationship that is mutually beneficial to both parties, and it helps if both people think that they are getting the better deal."

"But my question is 'how do you know when you have found the one?'" The girl finished up her sweeping and was discarding the debris off the porch and into the dead garden; all the while keeping eye contact with Kay.

The elder was thinking of how to delicately phrase her response. "How do you feel about him without thinking about it? How do you feel about him when you do think about it? If there is any negative thought there, then he is not the one. He could become the one with time, but until those feelings coincide as positive, don't take the plunge. Plus…you are far too young to get married."

"My two best friends are getting married this year", the girl insisted as if it held some merit.

Kay leaned forward in her chair and stared the girl in her face to animate the gravity of what she was going to say. The old lady paused and, in all seriousness, let out, "you are a half wit."

James sat awkwardly and uncomfortably in his shirt and tie. A local columnist was in his apartment; she was writing an article on the author who killed herself before her book was published. It was all very Sylvia Plath to the writer but James felt that was far too easy; he did the interview regardless. The columnist sat across from him in his messy apartment and laid a tape recorder down in front of him, "hope you don't mind, my notes are never very good", Sandy Macintosh admitted.

"No problem. I am used to it", he acknowledged.

"I bet you are", she continued, "so tell me something about Marie".

"You are going to have to be more specific than that", he insisted.

"Well, to start, why don't you tell me some things about her that made her."

"You are going to have to be more specific", he said uncomfortably adjusting his tie.

Sandy looked at him in disbelief but continued to pry regardless of her growing frustration, "Why don't you tell me why you loved her, maybe some things about her that you miss."

James sat for a moment before loosening his tie even more and clearing his throat in order to continue, "There are a few things I can think of."

Sandy sat up anxiously; "good, good, just talk away until you are done."

"Well to start, her smile. I will really miss that smile."

"What about it James?" The writer pressed for more detail.

James shut his eyes and leaned back on the couch as he continued, "she had a smile that made me love life, not because she was beautiful but because she made life beautiful, worth living. Especially when she would laugh at my jokes; she really thought I was funny and not many other people got me that way. She had these manly straggly hands that were always clammy but she was so soft. She loved a good high five and she was such a nerd, but in a way that people admired, she pulled it off well." James smiled and opened his eyes, "Marie had these nervous twitches, they were so annoying, drove everyone crazy. I miss them now."

Sandy nodded, she wasn't really getting what she was looking for out of this guy; she pushed on. "Why don't you tell me more about her personality, some details you remember about her that way?"

"I remember every detail; you are going to have to be more specific."

"Why don't you hone in on a couple things you liked about the way she used to act and a couple you didn't like."

James sat quietly for a minute before asking, "would you like some water or something?"

"I am fine thanks" Sandy responded.

"Okay then, the way she acted. Well when she was in a bad mood and snapped over something trivial and I gave her a look like 'are you kidding me', you could see the moment of realization when she came to terms that she was wrong. She didn't ever apologize, make excuses, but she would compose herself as if it never happened; it was so very her."

"Good" Sandy assured him, "stuff like that is good".

"She was extremely calculated. She was closed, precise and so meticulous. She rarely cried about things that mattered and if she did it was almost always in private. She always cried when she watched romantic comedies though; I always cried when I watched romantic comedies with her."

James leaned forward to light a cigarette. He gestured towards Sandy to offer her one but she shook her head with a smile on her face to politely say no thanks. He continued as he smoked, "I had no idea what to expect from her. I certainly had no idea what she would do next. Impressive mood swings, within a day she would snap at the smallest thing but get excited about something else. She would so smoothly move from ball of rage to happy kitten it was really incredible. At first I thought she was acting or playing a role but over a short time I came to terms with these changes and developed ways to deal with them. It changed from irritating to comforting for me; I was the only one who could deal with Marie and that made me worth something to her."

James paused as he toked on his cigarette and Sandy recognized this as an in, "To what did you attribute her mood swings?" James shook his head and put out his smoke in the ashtray. He knew what she wanted to hear; he knew what would make the article interesting.

"I don't know, maybe low blood sugar or something."

"Was she diabetic?" The writer asked.

"Wouldn't surprise me if she was", James replied confidently.

"Okay", Sandy said slowly with a confused look on her face.

"Can I ask you a question?" James requested, throwing Sandy off, but she nodded. "You are a writer right?"

"I like to think so."

"Do you annoyingly correct people's grammar all the time? Like when you are talking to someone and they say 'give that money to Pat and I', what would you say?"

"Nothing. What should I say?"

"Forget it. I was just curious." James said with a little disappointment.

"Was Marie pretty anal about grammar?"

"She could make anyone in the world think they are bad at grammar but she didn't do it to be right, she wanted you to learn, to see improvement in you. She loved improving people. There were some people, like her friend Lillian, that she thought were perfect, but that was rare. I was probably her biggest project." James paused trying not to let his eyes leak, "and look at me now. She would push people so hard to better themselves. She could be so harsh, but she was only that way with people she liked. She could always see a future that was better or greater than the one you could see. The future always had so much hope and potential when she let you see it through her eyes."

Sandy let James remain in this positive state for a few seconds before she added, "but she committed suicide."

"What does that have to do with anything?" James asked offensively.

"Her view of the future couldn't have been that good if she would rather die than live," She claimed with confidence.

"Why is it that writers can never write real but are only capable of a version of real?" James asked angrily.

"Life, in itself, is never interesting enough." Sandy asserted.

"Then you haven't been living it." James threw back at her, "Let's keep our focus here."

Sandy was irritated, but knew the truth in his comment. "Let's move on then shall we? My next question for you is which character from her book do you think most reflects her in real life?"

James smiled, wondering if the journalist sitting in front of him spouting off questions had even read the book. "She was a combination of the two; she taught herself most of life by watching others and the mistakes they made, and then she would try to relay her lessons learned to others."

"Okay, and did you like the book?" She asked expecting the typical answer.

James thought to himself and debated internally about whether or not to be honest. He was leaning more in one direction so he answered, "Everything changed when she finished the book. I guess, to answer your question, I hold a lot against it personally."

Sandy shuffled through her sheets of paper, looking for her question list, "I only have a few questions left and then I am out of your hair."

"Let's go then", James answered mildly impatiently.

"Do you know why she killed herself?"

"Yes I do".

"Will you tell me why?"

"No I won't."

"Do you accept why she did it?" she asked.

"My acceptance certainly doesn't matter at this point, but yes I do."

"Is there a connection between her death and the book?"

"Yes."

"Is there anything you would like to add?"

James took a moment before responding, "no". Sandy leaned over the table and turned off her tape recorder. "Thanks for your time", she said as she packed up and head for the door. She stopped, looking down at the ground, she bent down and picked up a bobby pin, "is this yours?" she asked with a smile. James walked to her and took it from her hand, "it is now."

Sandy could tell that she had over stayed her welcome; she let herself out. James stood where he was when he took the bobby pin from the reporter's hand. He was holding his hand out flat with the small metal contraption in his palm. He was reminded of one of Marie's fits.

James had just run home from work so that he could get ready for Marie's birthday party. When he came through the door he yelled to her, "I will only be five minutes and we can get out of here".

"I don't give a shit", was her reply.

He stopped in his tracks and shook his head while he walked back to the bedroom. Marie sat on the end of their bed in a beautiful black dress with her makeup and hair done perfectly. He dreaded asking but he did, "what's wrong?"

She looked up at him and started crying, "what is the point of this shit, I don't want to go."

"But you have to go, it is your party." James took a step towards her and she held her hand out telling him to stop. "What can I do to make you feel better?" he asked.

"You could fuck off", she said deliberately to hurt him.

"Marie, you look beautiful. You know that once you get there you won't feel depressed anymore because you will be with your friends."

"What the fuck do you know? You are always fucking happy and everyone loves you. Everyone feels sorry for you because you are with me. I hate my fucking life." She started taking out the bobby pins from her hair one by one and throwing them at James as hard as she could. "I don't feel beautiful James so why should I fake it?" she kept throwing the pins in his direction and when she ran out of pins she ripped at her hair and messed it beyond repair. "I don't have any fucking friends", she said as the tears streamed down her face catching her mascara and turning black.

James walked towards her and she started wailing her arms to slap him away and he firmly took her by the wrists and pulled her into him so that he could hug her. He held her tightly until she ceased to struggle and she broke down. She was wailing and trying to speak but he couldn't make out a single word she was saying aside from 'why' which she kept repeating.

After some time, he calmed her down and she looked at him and asked, "what are we going to do now?"

He smiled and reached down to the floor to pick up one of the hair pins that she had thrown and he stuck it in his hair and said, "I don't know about you but I am ready to go". They both started laughing and embraced. "I love you Marie", he whispered in her ear.

"I don't know why", she replied.

"Because without you in my life, I would have to buy cable television." She smiled and smacked him before she got up to pull herself together.

James didn't spend much time remembering the bad days now that she was gone. He lifted his head to look in the mirror across the hall from him. He took the bobby pin and stuck it into his short hair; it fell to the ground. He picked it up again from the floor and this time put forth more of an effort to figure out how to use the thing. He clipped it over his bangs and the weight on his hair made it hang over his forehead. He admired the new look in the mirror before he burst out laughing. "I can make anything look good", he joked to himself. The pin fell out of his hair again.

He did not pick it up. He stared at it lying on the floor; he felt it taunting him. His smile faded and his eyes welled up; he closed them to force the salty stream out into the open. "Things need to get better", he said to the hair pin that lay on the ground, "things need to get a lot better".

Jones searched through his pile of unopened bills for a government check that he may have missed coming through the mail. He tossed envelopes aside with frustration as he hunted. Nearing the end of the mountainous stack, he came across a familiar piece of tattered paper with his sister's chicken scratch handwriting scripted across it. He forgot about his plight and sat down, holding the paper in his hand and trying to make out the words that he had once memorized.

He remembered the day that she wrote this I.O.U. out to him; Jones thought to himself with a smirk, *who thought anyone would ever owe me*. He recalled a barely fifteen year old blond waif knocking so lightly on his door that he had only heard her by chance as he was getting a beer from the fridge at the time. When he opened the door he was more than surprised to see his little sister standing there looking oh so forlorn and he knew how desperate she must have been to talk because he hadn't seen her since the previous Christmas.

Jones towered over this young girl and she looked up at him hoping that he would invite her in without asking any questions. He invited her in nervously as he was hoping she wasn't there to ask him any personal questions. She took off her jacket and looked around for a place to hang it; due to Jones' circumstances she opted to hold onto it. She kept her shoes on and walked through her brother's disheveled, dirt filled, and airy apartment.

She wondered over to a large piece of scrap metal that Jones had started to weld and she stopped and stared. Jones smiled as he watched her head turn down towards her shoulder and then to the other shoulder as she tried to figure out what the form was going to become. She didn't dare ask what it was going to be because she didn't want her brother to think her to be young and ignorant as she most certainly was.

She turned to him and asked, "How are you?"

Relieved at the simplicity of the said question Jones released his breath and replied, "Same old."

Marie didn't know what the same old was for him but she did gather that it was a pretty simple and hedonistic lifestyle that he was leading. She longed to feel free from the world as her brother seemed to. She nodded as if she did know what 'same old' meant and the two stood silently staring at the other's feet. Jones thought that he would ask the question that was on both of their minds at this point, "so what brings you to this part of town? Does mom know you are here?"

"I just needed a change of pace I guess, thought I would see what you are doing now. No mom does not know that I am here, thought that would be best." Marie could feel her sweaty hands soaking through her jacket that she was gripping onto awkwardly as she searched for the right words to say. "Things are good though at home. Tomas is doing a little better in school and mom is the same."

"So things are terrible at home" he said bitterly.

"No," Marie answered immediately, "Now that it is just the three of us there is a lot less screaming and hardly any stuff being broken".

A twinge of guilt passed through Jones but it quickly passed; he lived life for himself now. "Do you want a beer?" he asked as he dug into the fridge for his own.

"I am fourteen", she replied.

"I was twelve when I started drinking" he said assuring her of his approval.

"I know what my weaknesses are going to be in life and I am in no rush to succumb to them", she said making her eldest brother feel like a very small man. She noticed that his ego had been affected and guilt overcame her. She tried not to cry but a tear escaped, "I didn't mean that personally, I am sorry."

Jones, confused and completely afraid of a woman's tears, consoled her from across the room, "it's okay, I don't really care…it doesn't bother me. You really don't need to cry, I am already over it", which he wasn't.

Marie broke down. She wept but covered her face with her jacket so her brother didn't have to look at her shame. She blurted out, "I don't know what to do anymore Jones. I can't seem to find any reason why I am alive. My life is passing me by and all I experience is depression and anger. Mom keeps telling me that I remind her of you…" She uncovered her face, "so I came here to see how I can make everything go away."

Jones stood absolutely frozen in fear. He had no idea what to say; he had no idea whether he should run in fear or throw his sister out the window. After brief consideration he decided to stutter intermittently and followed that up with some random questions. "Um, why would you think I would know how to make your pain go away?" he asked to begin. There was no reply. He continued, "do you think that this has something to do with your hormones or something?" She stopped crying but just looked at him blankly and said nothing. Nervously he couldn't stop talking, "Isn't there someone else you could talk to about this?"

Marie looked at her brother with disappointment on her face, "I thought you would understand me better. Did you really think about my options? Who would I go to, Matt, Connor or would you have me go to mom? Think about it Jones, you're the only one who wouldn't laugh me out the door."

He knew that she was right. Jones recognized this frustrated and disturbed demeanor from his past. He then focused on how to help her instead of how to get rid of her. This proved to be a beneficial switch for the two of them. He asked her some real questions like, "what makes you sad?" and "what makes you happy?" To which she replied "everything" and "nothing".

They talked back and forth for some time and the conversation lightened from the original subject. They talked about Jones' art and what inspires him to where he 'finds' his materials. They laughed together and when the day grew old it was time for her to go home despite the fact that no one even knew she was gone.

As she got up off her seat on the dusty floor, Jones had an idea, "what about art?" he asked her.

"What about it?" She asked him back.

"You were like a child prodigy. You used to go to those art classes and draw the most amazing things, why don't you get back into that?" he wondered out loud.

"I don't really like that anymore. I write poems sometimes now, but they aren't very good", she admitted.

"Marie, try everything artistic. Paint, write, sew, and see if there is anything that makes things better. When I left home I started painting but I wasn't very good at it so I started playing with metal and now that is all I ever want to do. Trust me, when you find an outlet it gives life reason."

Marie smiled and went on her toes to hug her brother, "this was exactly what I needed", she told him and it brought a smile to both of their faces. "I am just going to use the bathroom before I go," she said. Jones grabbed himself another beer and waited for his sister to evacuate. As she left he noticed her slip something onto his table; he didn't ask what.

When she left she thanked him again and the two were satisfied with the bond that had previously only consisted of a bloodline but now had become something more complex.

As Jones held the paper in front of him he deciphered the text and read it out loud, "I.O.U. a half decent conversation when you need it most."

Connor and James had sat across from each other for just over an hour drinking beer and talking about nothing more than what would be expected from two acquaintances passing quickly on the street. Connor was trying to engage him but James maintained his melancholic blank stare and one word answers. Connor's frustration got the better of him, "When are you going to let go Jay? She is gone and you have to move on."

James preserved his blank eyes and shook his head, "I will never let go", he said calmly. After a moment of thought James asked with little feeling in his voice, "how is it so easy for you? She was your sister; your baby sister."

Connor, without hesitation, replied "She killed herself. She chose to die. No one is to blame but her. Do you think it makes sense to mourn; no; to worship someone who knowingly jumped off a cliff? Do you?"

James thought that he should be mad at his friend though he wasn't. He knew the whole story and Connor didn't. "Connor, you sound like her when you talk like that."

"Dude you need to come back to the land of the living. You can't follow her anymore."

Connor asserted.

"I don't want to follow her; I want to feel like I did with her. I only have the memories and they are fading no matter how hard I try to keep them. You would be the same way if you lost Lil. You would." James was starting to feel some frustration surfacing; it was a nice change from the normal nothing.

Connor, feeling a little buzzed and seeing that James was getting a little riled thought he would keep taunting him. "Lil would never be so selfish to do what Marie did. My wife would never abandon me or her life." As he finished saying those cutting words he tipped his drink back and finished his beer. By the look on James' face he could tell he had gone too far. James said nothing but he looked forward as if deep in thought, his face turning bright red with anger and his eyes welling against his will.

James opened his mouth to say something but held off for a few moments thinking before he blankly stated, "she had cancer."

The two sat drinking their beers both absorbing what was just said.

Connor looked at him, now making eye contact, and he laughed "No she didn't". He waited for James to verify that that was a bad joke; no verification came."

James added, "She did, I assure you. Ovarian cancer, and right before she died they found a tumor in her brain. Still funny?"

Connor was feeling ill; he put on his coat and head for the door. James put his own winter coat on, threw some money down on the table and grabbed Connor's mittens and handmade wool toque. He left the bar and tripped over Connor who was sitting on the stairs outside smoking a cigarette. James sat down in the hardened snow pile beside the man who drove him to betray Marie's last wish.

James knew that it was going to take some time for Connor to accept the news so he opted to release some pain he had, until this point, kept to himself. "Watching someone you love die is hard. Watching someone you love pretend they're not dying is impossible. Do you know how hard it was to watch her wince in pain when people turned their heads just to flash a smile when they looked back again? I was the only person she told, but when she would lay in bed next to me she would turn away to hide her tears." James wiped his own tears with Connors mitten and continued, "She hurt like I have never seen anyone hurt. There was nothing I could say to convince her to share her burden." James started to feel some pressure releasing from his chest as he revealed her secret. It was killing him to hold it in for so long listening to people scorn her. Connor offered him a smoke and he accepted.

As he exhaled Connor said "she didn't have to do that. We would have supported her. She didn't have to be alone."

"She didn't want to spend the end of her life having you smile at her and laugh at her jokes when you normally wouldn't have. She wanted you, and everyone, to treat her exactly as they always had." James explained.

"We would have, nothing would have changed." Connor contested as he lit another cigarette.

James laughed at his ignorant friend. "You are telling me that if your little sister had cancer, was bent over in agony and dying, you would still give her a hard time? Would you have made fun of her and told her what a baby she was being? Would you make fun of her being sick all the time and would you tell her suck it up and get over it? Trust me when I say that I know you wouldn't have. I couldn't treat her the same way and she knew it; and she hated it."

Connor lowered his head and dropped his forehead into the palms of his hands. He shook his head back and forth and let out a loud irritated grunt. "She could have told me. I loved her, she should have told me."

"I honestly think she lasted as long as she did because she had to keep up the façade of relative wellness. She had to be strong and it made her stronger."

Connor, with his head still in his hands, asked with nervous comprehension, "So that is why she jumped. That's why she did it."

James nodded.

"Why didn't you tell me she was going to do that? I could have said goodbye. If I had known I could have stopped her." Connor asserted angrily. He looked up at the sky and watched the snow falling ever so delicately down from the sky; just a polite warning of the storm to follow.

James, slightly offended replied, "Don't you think I would have tried to stop her if I knew. I didn't know when she was going to do it. I didn't really know if she would do it; I just guessed that she might."

Connor knew why James would guess such a thing, "because someone with such control issues would never let her fate be sealed by a disease that she had no control over."

"Yeah," James responded, "Something like that."

The two stood and Connor put on the rest of his winter gear. They started walking up the street because the sidewalks weren't shoveled. There was silence between them. James listened to the quiet of a winter street with the exception of one man getting a head start shoveling his walkway. One block closer to home Connor said with anger," I just can't fuck believe she didn't tell me! How could she keep this from all of us?"

"With great difficulty, dedication and pain", James said with aggravated patience.

They continued their journey home and both stepped silently in thought. "When did she find out?" asked Connor.

"She kept it from me for a while so I don't know exactly" answered James. "I honestly couldn't believe that you guys didn't notice."

"She was always sick man; there was always something with her. To be honest, Lil and I thought she was pregnant for the last few months, with the nausea and she was always so tired" Connor wiped a tear from his face. He didn't want to talk about this anymore.

"She counted on that Connor, don't feel bad about it. She knew you wouldn't question her having an ulcer, or the random infections she claimed to have. She thought that you guys would suspect pregnancy which is why she started wearing looser clothing to sway you even more. She planned it all, you had to believe it." James stopped walking as this was the point where the two went in two separate directions.

"Fuck that pisses me off." Connor asserted. "I can't believe I was outsmarted by my sister."

James laughed noticing Connor's humor surfacing. The two men hugged in the solemn snow filled street. "I better go tell Lillian the news." Connor said as he tapped his friend on the back. They walk off in different directions.

James was feeling the cold set in now as he made his way down the snowy street in his running shoes. The snow was falling harder than before. He looked back to see if Connor was still within sight; he wasn't.

James stopped and approached a tall snow bank at the side of the road. He turned so that he was facing away from the curb. He shut his eyes and jumped backwards into pile. He fell into the snow and felt joy for the first time since she left him. He lay there, dressed inappropriately, almost completely covered in snowfall. He smiled as he looked up at the sky and watched the snow falling to the earth; a calm he had forgotten fell over him.

The last time he lay in the snow she was beside him holding his hand. He looked to his right, as he did the last time, but she wasn't beside him. He closed his eyes picturing her playfully laughing with him and he smiled as he would have then. Then he took a sobering deep breath, quickly got up and ran home to find a different kind of warmth.

*K*ay sat down after an uncontrollable coughing fit. The young girl helped her down to the chair; she was very nervous that the cough was more than her elder let on. She asked, knowing the answer, "are you okay?"

"Of course I am, what the hell is wrong with you?" Kay said vengefully.

"Nothing, it just seems as though you may be sicker than you are telling me", the girl responded.

"Why would I hide being sick, that doesn't even make sense," questioned the geriatric.

"Because you are a pride filled, thick skulled, 'pretend I am not sick when I really am' kind of gal."

"What are you looking for me to say right now?" Kay asked frustrated at the girl's intuition.

"I am looking for you to tell me the truth. I am looking for you to admit that you aren't undefeatable. Most of all, I am looking for you to admit that you are suffering; that you suffer everyday and not only physically." The girl went to the bathroom to get a cold cloth for Kay's warm head before she could respond intuitively to the previous comment. Kay sat alone in the kitchen, helpless in her chair. The girl was wrong, her cough was nothing more than a cough; but she was suffering, she was suffering every day. Kay tried to get up but was paralyzed with pain. The cancer had spread, not that a doctor had told her but she could feel it moving through her body. "The end is near" she muttered to herself.

"Don't be so negative", the girl added walking into the room, "is it an infection or something?"

"You could say that" Kay responded.

"But you wouldn't?" The youth sat in the chair beside her elder and placed her hands on Kay's. She felt how fragile this strong woman had become and it broke her heart. "Please tell me if you know there is something wrong with you."

"Just because it is the end of the beginning doesn't mean it is the beginning of the end." Kay said.

"What does that mean?" Girl asked with tears in her eyes.

"It means that I am going to die; everyone does. But that doesn't end anything for you. Just because people die…it doesn't mean anything at all." Kay uttered trying not to grip her stomach as it sent messages of pain to her brain, "there is no more wrong with me than there usually is."

The girl forced the elderly woman to look into her eyes. "I know it is hard for you to share and I know it is hard for you to show weakness, but please, talk to me. I will never forgive you if I find out that you are carrying a burden that we could share."

Kay looked deep into her eyes, smiled honestly and said, "I promise you one thing: If I knew I was going to die of some tragic disease, I would tell you, I swear to you." The girl, seeing truth in her eyes, was convinced of the verity in her words, "thank you Kay".

"No problem. Now get out of here so I can take a nap"

"A nap? Isn't that a little too senior citizen for you?" she asked.

"It is a new thing I am trying out," Kay admitted.

"Okay I will stop by tomorrow", the girl assured her.

"See you then."

The girl left and locked the door behind her; Kay remained in the kitchen questioning timing. She smiled to herself and shed a few tears knowing what all of this meant. Kay thought of how she was left behind to remember all those she had loved; this girl was the only one left to remember her. This girl was everything.

Lillian avoided eye contact with her husband in order to make him feel more comfortable talking about his sister and the information he received the week before. She was thinking back to recollect if there had been any dead giveaways that she might have missed that screamed 'I am Marie and I am dying of cancer'; she laughed out loud.

Connor shot her a glare and asked, "what could be so funny?"

With a smile Lillian reminded him, "remember the New Years before she died, remember your beautiful speech? You were going on about how the coming year was going to be great for all of us because you just had an eerie feeling about it". She laughed again, "You literally went on about prosperity and how great life was for like ten minutes; you got so upset because Marie and James were looking at each other and seeming so sad and you thought they were in a fight and ruining the night. I bet they were just thinking about the inevitable outcome of her life and how brutal what you were saying was."

Connor, unimpressed but incapable of foreseeing the black humour in his speech, cracked a smile and continued, "Yeah, how ironic is a celebration of new beginnings when you know it is all going to end, and miserably?"

"After your speech she hugged you and with a huge smile on her face she toasted to you" Lillian added, "she said the only way her life could improve was if you moved to Afghanistan but left me behind so she could have me full time."

"Yeah", Connor said hesitantly, "she did say that." He shed a happy tear and quickly wiped it away, "She was such a good fucking liar".

"You hated that about her," she said.

"Now I kinda respect her for it; I like the memories I have of her, even the ones I used to hate", Connor admitted.

Lillian leaned over and kissed her husband on his top lip, "I am going to get ready for bed baby and before we go to bed I need to talk to you about your brother Matt". Connor nodded and focused his attentions back to his book and she got up and went into the bathroom to take off her makeup.

She wiped her face with a white wash cloth and as she took it down from her eyes she peered at her reflection in the mirror. "I really like how you finished your story", she said, "I don't know if you pay any attention to me anymore because I haven't been talking to you lately. I need you to know that you are much smarter, stronger and hilarious than I ever knew you to be. I hope that things work out for you in death like you made them work out in life. I don't know if I will ever talk to you again so, if I don't, thank you for not telling us that you were leaving."

She smiled to herself and closed her eyes tightly and her tears fell down her face. She poured cold water over the cloth and placed back over her eyes so the evidence would disappear; Lillian had taken a page from the book of the dead.

Jones approached his younger brother's house trying to sort out what to say in such a time. He could see from a block away that the lights were on and that Matt was on the porch rocking back and forth and their big cushy swing. He approached the bottom step and stood their respectfully waiting for an invitation from the man he was going to scorn. He also noticed that Matt was drinking what looked like whiskey with no ice nor mix.

"When was the last time you had a drink little brother?" asked Jones trying to break the silence.

"Dunno, a while", was the curt reply. "Why are you here?"

Jones remained at the bottom of the stairs determined not to be an intruder. He scratched his head like a cartoon character might when they can't figure something out. "Well, let me tell you. Josie was talking to Lillian earlier who, then, talked to Connor. Connor called me and I drew the short stick so I walked and hour and a half over here to talk to you."

"Seems like a lot of talking", Matt said sarcastically.

"Yep. A lot of talking indeed. Now I am here waiting to be invited up so we can talk some more."

"Great. Can't wait." Matt gestured for him to come up and sit down. Jones did just that. Matt continued, "I only have one glass out here with this bottle of Glenfiddich. We will have to share the glass or one of us can just drink out of the bottle."

"Or I could go inside and grab another glass", Jones said thinking that to be reasonable suggestion.

"Can't go inside. Josie is going to be on the phone and doesn't want to see me right now. Doubt she wants to see you either."

Jones leaned back in his chair and nodded in agreement. He wondered if he should get right into it or if he should let Matt talk when he was ready. So he lead with, "What the fuck are you doing?"

"Fuck off", Matt said, "fuck you."

"I am serious".

"So am I".

"When is it exactly you are supposed to leave?" Jones asked.

"Two weeks." Matt passed his brother the glass and topped it up with the bottle before he took a drink straight from it.

"That's fucked up bro."

Matt laughed, "I only have one glass".

"I meant that you are going to abandon your family completely and on top of that you gave her two week's notice. Having a family is not like having a job, you can't just quit."

His smile disappeared. "Who the hell are you to tell me what's fucked up? You do whatever the fuck you want. You left all of us at home with mom the second you could bail. You move around all the time and don't tell anyone until after you have gone. Dude, you don't even have a fucking bed. That's fucked up."

Jones, being a much stronger, well built version of his younger brother, grabbed Matt by his chin and forced him to look him in the eyes. "You little shit. You are leaving your fucking wife and child to pursue your own selfish indulgences. Do you know who you are? Do you know how sad this is?"

Matt's eyes welled up with tears knowing very well that he had just been compared to his father, a man he has desperately sought to impress his entire life. He pulled his head away from Jones and wiped his eyes. "I can't do this anymore. I can't live this life, I am going crazy. I need to do more."

"You can do more Matt, just do it with your family."

"I can't Jones," he said shaking his head. "I have made up my mind."

"I can't believe you could do this to Amelie when you have lived through it. Dad destroyed us when he left."

"He didn't give a fuck about us. He still doesn't."

"Exactly!" Jones said allowing some anger to surface, "look at you. You are telling your daughter that you don't give a fuck. She is going to be raised alone with her mother thinking that her daddy doesn't give a fuck about her. She is going to grow up bitter and disjointed like all of us. Way to go."

"Fuck off. Go home."

"You fuck off." Jones calmly sipped from his rock glass and thought of something to say that may be going overboard. He couldn't help himself, "I would say that Marie was a fine example of what can happen to a little girl with no father. She jumped off a fucking cliff when she was in her prime. You want Amelie to jump off a cliff someday brother?"

Matt turned to face Jones, "did you just fucking say that? What the hell is wrong with you?" He rubbed his eyes with both his hands and looked back up, "our sister was obviously pretty messed up mentally to do what she did. Please don't ever compare my daughter to her again."

"Just calling it like I see it. You have no idea what sort of damage you can do to a child by leaving them. Well, actually, you have a very good idea. To this day you keep arranging dinners for him that he doesn't come to and I bet it breaks your heart a little every time."

"I am tired of this Jones, please leave."

Jones nodded, he didn't want to become preachy and he was pretty sure that he got his point across. He placed his glass down on the deck and stood up, towering about his seated brother. "Please tell me that you will reconsider. Or at least that you will consider reconsidering."

Matt nodded to appease him but had zero intention of following through. He had made up his mind. He wanted to live life for himself and not other people. He didn't care how many people he would lose in the process. Jones had descended the stairs and Matt, in his drunkenness thought that was the reason he should share, "I want to live for myself and not other people."

Jones stopped walking and turned around, "what was that?"

Matt cleared his throat, "I said that I want to live my life for me and not for other people."

His older brother nodded in his distant sort of way and replied, "I could see that, it does run in our family. Dad left because he was so self-absorbed. Mom still drinks herself stupid because that is a life she prefers despite the effects on others. Marie killed herself because that was the best thing for her. It is sad that you are going to follow in suit. What about the people who don't just care about themselves, the people who share their life with others. What about Connor and Tomas? They are going to lose another sibling within a year. What about your wife? You are leaving all of us just like the people who have hurt you." Jones laughed sadly, turned around and walked away; there was nothing left to say.

Matt yawned and curled up on the swing feeling sorry for himself while Josie cried inside feeling more alone than she ever had before.

James knew that he had betrayed one of Marie's last wishes by admitting her defeat to her brother but he felt as if the weight of the world had been lifted from his shoulders. He wasn't like her, he couldn't bare a burden to save someone else from it unless he could have done it for her. She had made sure that he would never have to be burdened while she lived; why would she wish it upon him in death? He decided that she knew the whole time that he would share her secrets; he was weak and that was a personality trait of his that would never falter.

He grabbed his jacket and a book from the book case, her favorite, Jitterbug Perfume. He took it out onto the fire escape and sat watching the people below. He felt free for the first time since he met her, free of responsibility. He enjoyed this new air until the guilt of how he broke the news to Connor overcame him. James knew how harsh he had been because he was angry at the time. He managed to forgive himself; Marie had been pretty curt with the news herself.

James leaned over the couch and brushed Marie's hair away from over her closed eyes. He kissed her on the forehead and nudged her to wake her but she didn't move. He delicately slid his arms underneath her back and legs. He bent his knees as not to hurt his back and he lifted her up to take her to bed as he did so many times before. He lifted her but he stood still realizing the gravity of her situation. He carried her into their bedroom and gently placed her onto their bed. He sat beside her playing with her hair and thinking. He wiped his eye; she was already disappearing. "I have done everything your doctors told me to", he said to her, "why won't you get better?"

She said nothing; she slept. "I wish you would be stronger. I know you have given up." He laid down beside her and rolled his hands over ribs which he could distinctly feel through his t shirt that she was wearing.

"Do you want to die?" he asked her curiously. She slept; he knew the answer.

He reached over her to her daily medication to get her to take it but as he lifted over her sleepy head he recognized that there was nothing left in the bottle. He put it back down and reached for her blue pills and that bottle was empty too; the big pills, small white pills and even smaller pink pills were empty as well. He took a moment to convince himself that this didn't mean what he thought it did. He got up from the bed and went to the kitchen to pour himself a drink. He reached for the whiskey that she hated so he could always manage to keep some in the house and he poured himself a large glass, no ice.

He drank it. He poured himself another; he drank it. He began to realize why she drank; it makes difficult easy. He decided that he could no longer be okay with this situation.

James marched confidently into their room with something on his mind. He shook her more aggressively than he needed to. She made an angry face and mumbled, "go away, I'm sleeping".

"Wake up", James asserted, "wake up!" He jumped up and down on the bed until she opened her eyes and lifted herself up, smirking as she stared at him jumping around like an idiot.

"What's up?" She asked him patiently, knowing he wouldn't wake her unless it was an emergency or he was drunk.

"I have something to say" he said with such conviction as he halted the bouncing.

Marie laughed realizing that it was no emergency, "what's up hardcore? Did you go drinking after work or did you hit the whiskey because you were thinking too much?"

James, irritated at such flagrantly true assumptions, "NO", he proclaimed, "I just have something to say".

"What's that?" she asked ready to fall back asleep.

"I am sick of you being sick. I am tired of you being tired."

"Am I killing you because I'm dying?" Marie smiled at her own wit.

"That's not funny Marie. You need to stop giving up now. Please just stay with me." He knelt beside her in the bed, took her hand and kissed it as if he was kissing her better.

"James..." she paused and he stared at her awaiting her response. "James I am worse than before. I am not giving up on my body, it is giving up on me." She pulled him closer to her and they kissed. "The cancer has spread; I have a tumor in my brain. I am dying faster than I can pretend to live. I am sorry I couldn't tell you."

James sat on the bed motionless, "how long?"

"Not long enough" she replied calmly.

"You have accepted this already then?" He asked.

"I have had more than one opinion and I have accepted that this is something that is going to happen despite how much I smile for you."

He sat without touching her and thought about how hurt he was. "Why didn't I go with you? Why wouldn't you tell me how bad it was getting?"

Marie started to cry; he wiped her tears because she was too proud to. She looked into his beautiful honest eyes, "Because your hope was the only thing I had left to keep me alive. I couldn't take that away from either of us." He took her in his arms and squeezed her harder than he should have but she loved it, she needed it.

Marie waited a moment before pulling away and she laid back down and reached out for his hand which he willfully gave to her. She continued, "I am going to sleep now, please don't take it personally, I am just very tired."

James nodded, leaned down and kissed her soft lips. "Good night Marie. I love you."

Her smile faded as she slipped out of consciousness.

James held on for a minute before he went to the kitchen to further numb himself with the remaining whiskey. He forgot almost everything within an hour and slipped comfortably into bed to spoon with the love of his life.

Tomas finished the dinner that June had left him in her fridge that day with a note and a smiley face to brighten his day; he certainly had never been exposed to such pleasantries growing up. He warmed it in the microwave and took it outside to eat on the deck. One of the neighbors waved to him and warned him of an incoming storm to which he acted very concerned about before he disappeared behind the fence.

He couldn't stand life's pleasantries, especially when people knew he had been removed from his home and his alcoholic mother and they reflected that knowledge in their voice when they spoke to him. He stuck a fork full of mashed potatoes into his mouth. As he swallowed them whole he looked to the sky and recognized something that you always know when you grow up on a farm; a storm was coming. "I always think of you now when there's a storm; but you know that don't you?" He packed some turkey down his throat when he felt the first drop of rain on his arm. He ate faster, racing the rain; he wouldn't be driven away. He won the race as he shoveled the last bite into his mouth and the drops of rain became more significant and adamant.

He sat unyielding, with his eyes closed he faced the sky and rain fell hard onto his face washing away the remnants of food that had been left behind as he rushed through his meal. He thought about the news that Connor told him about Marie. She had taught him to love the rain; a lesson that he would always remember.

Brother and sister sat on the covered porch together, each with a beer in hand watching the dark clouds roll across the sky. "It's like heaven on earth" Marie said mesmerized by the reigning darkness.

Tomas asked his sister, "Why do you love the storm so much?"

"I don't know" she replied.

Tomas laughed, "mom always said you sat in the rain because it would hide your tears when you cried. She also said that you were crying because you were feeling sorry for yourself for being alive." The two of them smiled.

Marie shook her head, "mom is a bitch. But it is nice to see you being honest"

"Yep" Tomas agreed. They sat in silence, as they so often had before.

"Can you hear that Tom?" She asked with a whisper.

"Hear what?" he asked listening intently.

"Shhhhh" she held a finger up to silence him. He looked out towards the fields and then back at her; she had shut her eyes. He could hear it. It was the sound of a downpour that had not yet hit them. He watched her smile crawl across her face and he shut his eyes as well. He could feel the rain storming across the corn coming towards them; his heart started racing. He opened his eyes when Marie grabbed his hand and pulled him and said, "come on!"

He got up out of the wicker chair and followed her. At first she was walking but that quickly turned into a run. She was heading for the field and he ran after her. "What are you doing?" He screamed after her.

Marie yelled back at him with her hands in the air, "I am meeting it halfway!"

Tomas laughed and as he reached the edge of the corner the rain hit him like a wall. He laughed and continued to run as the adrenaline was also hitting him with full force. He stopped and admitted defeat to the torrential downpour. He called out, "Marie! Where are you?" He could hear a distant reply so he ran in that direction. "Where are you?" he called out. He ran in the direction of her voice.

He came closer and closer but he had lost himself in the corn and he wasn't really sure where he was anymore. He just kept calling out to his sister and following her voice. The rain didn't give in. He finally came back to the clearing by the house. He was now drenched from head to toe. He took a step closer to the house when he noticed that Marie was on the porch drinking a beer. He ran up the stairs and saw that she was barely wet. "What are you doing?" He asked her curiously.

"Drinking a beer on the porch", she replied. "What the hell are you doing out there running around in a cornfield in the rain?"

"I thought I was following you. Why did you come in?" he asked a little irritated.

"It started to rain. I didn't want to get hit by lightening or ruin my shoes", she replied with a smile as she passed Tomas a fresh cold beer. He sat down and looked out at the land as water poured from the sky; it was beautiful.

"You didn't answer my question" he said, "why do you love a storm so much? You have to admit that it is weird that you avoid the sun and love the rain." He leaned back in his chair and focused his attention on to her so that she would feel pressure to answer.

Marie felt the pressure and thought out her answer before she gave it. "Tom, do you know that feeling of excitement you get when you finish your last final exam or when you have your first kiss with a girl? Well that how I feel before a rain. I feel like I could do anything, like I could be anyone. I feel different." She took a sip from her beer and Tomas waited knowing that she had more to say. "I hate the sun, it hurts skin, my eyes, it makes me sweat. The rain washes all of the discomfort away and soothes the pain. The rain protects me."

Tomas laughed and added, "It hides your tears too, don't forget that."

"That it does Tommy, it does indeed," she answered sarcastically. "But the greatest thing about a storm is after the rain." She stopped.

Tomas didn't wait long before asking, "What about after the rain?"

"Isn't it obvious?"

"Obviously not," he replied smartly.

"Well, little brother, after the rain the world is a new one. The rain has replenished everything. That silence in the streets that comes after a storm is only comparable to the silence that follows a great death. People are usually mourning a sunny day when they should love the rain that saved them. Sunshine is grossly overrated."

Her little brother smiled and replied, "We can tan in the sun, it gives us vitamins and other good stuff."

"It gives us cancer." Marie said in a way that was considered witty sarcasm at the time but now Tomas knew was bitterness towards an unyielding adversary.

Tomas picked up his plate that was now pooled with water. He wiped his sopping brow with his sleeve and he turned to the house. June was pulling in the driveway as he opened the door and now he knew he would have to explain his presence in the rain; or he would just play it off as a thing that kids do when they grow up with an alcoholic. That was working for him so far. He had never guessed that his situation would ever have any benefits.

Samson clung the phone to his ear and stood silently as he thought about what James had just told him. He waited before continuing, "so that is why she did it. That is why she stopped." James explained Marie's condition before she died and then waited a few minutes to let Samson absorb things before excusing himself from the call. Samson said goodbye, hung up the phone and took a seat at his kitchen table.

He couldn't believe the news. He was trying to disprove James but the more he thought about it the more it made sense to him. It explained so much when he recalled the last time that he saw her.

Marie lay on the couch wondering what ridiculous day time television she would choose to entertain her today. James had spent a lot of money he didn't have to pay for a satellite so that she could watch movies everyday instead of junk; the junk made Marie feel better about herself and her life. She flipped from channel to channel and laughed at herself, she looked like a girl going through her first break up, still in her house coat with a blanket over her watching talk shows to get her through the pain; her pain was physical but the concept was the same.

She heard a song on a commercial and leaned forward to her notebook to write its title down. Before she could put the pen down there was a knock at the door. She wasn't expecting anyone but she knew that the knocker was expecting to see her.

"Who is it?" she called out. She couldn't make out the muffled response but she did recognize the voice, "come in" she yelled as best she could. Samson opened the door and quickly shut it behind him. He smiled at her but said nothing. He kicked his shoes off and then neatly tucked them against the wall; Marie knew by his entrance that she was going to have to start lying to him. He approached the couch while taking off his jacket and he sat, placing his coat behind him.

"Marie", he said kindly, "I just ran into your coworker Adam and he was wondering why you quit your job." He smiled at her and continued, "I was shocked that you had quit but even more so when he let me know that you quit your job three months ago." He paused momentarily, Marie thought it might be to contain his rage, but soon he continued, "I am here because I need you to tell me what's going on. You have never lied to me and I know that if you did, that there would be a very good reason for it. Why have you been pretending to work? Why did you quit your job? What are you guys using for money? What is going on? Are you sick? You look terrible."

Marie laughed at his questioning because he was beginning to sound like her. She put her hand on his as she collected her thoughts. "I hated my job. James told me that he would rather me stay home happy then go to work miserable. I didn't want anyone to know because you know how judgmental the boys can be and plus I wanted to write full time and no one takes that seriously. As far as money goes, we have none, less than none actually but I did get approved for a sizable loan that should take care of us for a few months at least. Yes, I am sick, I have a lung infection and a hangover; you don't look so hot yourself. Was there anything I missed?"

Samson did have a few questions left in him, "I thought you had already finished your book and found a publisher, have you started another one? And if you guys are so poor don't you think it is a little silly that you have such extravagant cable? If you are hung over then why wasn't I invited out last night? Lastly, you didn't explain why you lied to me."

"I have always loved you because you are impossible to distract." Marie told him before answering his list of questions. "I am done the rewrites of my book and your final copy is in the bedroom in an envelope with your name on it, thank you for looking it over. The cable is for James so he can watch European football; he has always been high maintenance. Last night was just me getting drunk alone to try to become inspired for book two."

Samson took his hand away from under hers and leaned back against the arm of the couch, "and?"

"I lied to you", she stated bluntly as she nodded her head in agreement with herself, "but I had to."

"Why?" Samson asked. He was crushed that he had caught her in a lie because he thought their relationship was far beyond such simplicities.

Marie bounced back and forth between the truth and a lie in her head. It devastated her to deceive him but he was going to interrupt her plan if she told him the whole truth. She kept with the plan, "honestly Sam I didn't think you would approve."

"Approve of what?" he inquired curiously.

"I know what you think of me and how far you think I will go and I didn't want you to think less of me because I don't have a job. I know that you will say it doesn't matter but that it really will matter in your head." Marie waited with abated breath anticipating what his next move would be.

Samson said nothing and watched her reaction; he knew how silence tortured her. He didn't know that she was now burdened by a much worse torture. He broke the silence, "well I am sorry that you think that because it is far from true."

In relief she replied, "I am glad to hear that." They sat silently and she deliberated for a moment, "I want you to know something Samson". He nodded to acknowledge that he was listening and she continued, "the last person in this world that I would ever want to hurt is you."

He smiled and quickly contested, "aren't you forgetting someone?"

"No", she told him, "I have hurt him more than I can believe a person can forgive another. You, Samson, I have made an enormous effort to maintain a friendship with. It isn't always easy for me due to my inability to control my cruelty sometimes but you have been a friend to me. You should have a statue erected in your honor to celebrate how generous you are, how understanding you can be, how beautiful your heart is."

Samson interjected, "I forgive you for the lie you don't have to go crazy with the uncharacteristic compliments."

Marie propped herself up, reached for his face and turned it so he was forced to look into her eyes. "Samson, my whole life I have lived but I never knew what friendship was before you. Without you asking me for new chapters to read I couldn't have finished the book as fast as I did. Without your encouragement I couldn't have graduated nor would I have an urge to own property in order to build equity, just don't tell anyone I said that. I adore you but I cry for you because you can't see yourself the way I do."

Samson sat still and Marie's hand dropped from his face because she was too tired to hold it up. He thought that she was losing interest in this conversation. He couldn't pretend anymore and he needed at least one answer, "do you love me Marie?"

"Sam, I have loved you since the moment I met you. I have respected you, admired you, and learned from you."

Samson looked down at her blanketed feet that lay in from of him; he wanted to touch them but thought it might be inappropriate. "You don't love me like I want you to", he said holding back a self piteous tear.

Marie's heart broke because he didn't understand her circumstances, "I do love you that way Sam, I always have, but timing has not been a friend of ours. I love James and he has been too wonderful to me. I don't think that you would like the future that I have to offer, it is full of dark times."

"James loves you; he may or may not love you more than I do. I think that I could take anything that came my way though."

"Yeah" Marie agreed verbally but not mentally, "I am sure you could."

"But I am not going to am I?" he asked.

"Not if I can help it," she said honestly.

Samson got up to hide his disappointment in the conversation. He put his jacket on and head for the door. Marie knew what sadness she was inflicting on him but she couldn't betray herself for him. She called to him as his hand touched the door handle, "Sam wait". He stopped and turned towards her.

"What's up?" he asked hopeful yet seemingly detached. He watched as his usually lively and beautiful friend struggled to get up from the seated position in order to talk to him. *That infection must be bad* he thought to himself. "You don't have to get up", he assured her.

Marie was a very stubborn woman who rarely accepted reality for what it was so she insisted on being the strong one here. She threw the blanket onto the couch and slowly walked over to her old friend. She held her arms out asking him for a hug and he complied; they embraced but Samson noted that he could barely feel her touch him. She pushed him out and told him, "if you are patient, you will understand some things about me that are hard for me to explain. You are going to hate me, you are going to love me, but all I want from you is to remember me and the friendship we have now."

"Trust me that I have tried to forget you and failed", he joked but then remembered the finished copy of her book "I am going to grab that last draft", he said to her.

"Sure it is on my desk in the bedroom with your name on it" she guided him. "The faster you get that to me the better, I would like to start sending copies out on Monday."

He came back towards her with the package in hand, "have you decided on a title yet?"

"I have", she said, "but it is less mind blowing and more just what the book is about".

"Well", he waited, "what is it?"

"Conversations with Kay", she replied.

"You have always loved alliteration, it's perfect", Samson assured her.

"Thank you", she said appreciatively as the title was not so well received from James.

"That's why I'm here".

"I know", she said and gave him one last hug. Samson noticed that she wasn't pulling away like she usually did. He enjoyed the prolonged embrace but, before it ended, he panicked. He took her boney shoulders in his hands and held her stiffly forcing more eye contact, "are you really okay?" He watched her hesitation in response and repeated, "are you okay, please tell me the truth."

Marie stood still for a mere moment before she guaranteed him, "I am fine! You know how I am when I am hung over; I don't know what's going on!" She sealed the lie with a seemingly genuine smile and even threw in a, "now get lost and let me suffer in peace."

"Okay", said her friend believing that alcohol was to blame for her state. "Call me later; now that I know you are unemployed I am going to want to see you more often."

"Obviously", she replied, "who wouldn't? That's why I need to keep it quiet."

They kissed each other on the cheek and Samson left feeling much more confident than when he had arrived.

Marie shut the door and made her way over to the couch where her blanket and pillow awaited her return. She took the phone off of the coffee table and dialed James' cell phone with no answer; she left a short message, "James, I think I just said goodbye to Samson and it was strange. Wake me when you get home so we can talk about it." She hung up the phone and laid her head on the pillow facing the television. Her eyes tried to resist closing but the fatigue won this fight, she fell asleep and had confusing dreams that were guided by the soap operas on television at that time.

Lillian walked down the cool empty street both elated and confused. She touched her stomach knowing that this time it was different; it was now a fortress. Her thoughts were skipping frantically; how would she tell Connor; what were they going to do for money; was this the best time; was she happier than she was scared? She turned the corner and entered a park where she and Marie used to meet for their 'talks'. She approached the swing set where they would, with all of their best efforts, try to swing higher than the other; she sat alone on the middle swing.

She pushed off and swung back and forth with very little effort. She wondered how motherhood would be. It was a great responsibility, she decided. Lillian recognized that her new found responsibilities of caring for the family since Marie died would come in handy. She laughed out loud wondering if Connor and his brothers would write her references; not that you need references to have a child but that maybe you should.

Lillian pushed harder off the ground to gain some height on her upswing. She got higher and then higher still, wondering if she would fall off. Smiling to herself she thought about her lost friend, realizing that Marie was, all along, the parent that kept everything from falling apart.

When she felt that she might be putting the pea inside her in danger, Lillian stopped trying to swing higher. She stopped and stared at the ground, focusing on the past instead of her future. She thought about the conversation that she had with her sister in law that made her realize that Marie was actually human. It was August, quite a few years ago, and Marie had sounded nervous and asked her to meet her by the swing set.

Lillian had left immediately after receiving the phone call asking her to meet Marie at the park but her friend was already there waiting on the middle swing, she was trying to swing left and right like the swing didn't want to.

Lillian wasn't ten feet from her before asking "what's going on sista?"

Marie looked up at her and declared, "we need to talk about the nonsense that is going on inside my head. I need you to sort this out for me; you are the only one who can."

She laughed before replying, "well I have sorted a lot of your nonsense before, what type am I dealing with this time?"

"Love. I think. Or something else. I don't really know, that's why I am here. You know stuff, and, hopefully you can sort this out for me."

She laughed, "Um, Okay. But you realized you just said the L word right?"

"That's the problem", Marie said, "I think I am in love and I need you to tell me how to stop feeling so awful."

"That's doesn't sound like love. Love is not a bad thing."

"Look, ever since I have met this man I have felt nothing but confusion, nausea, hope, excitement and nausea. I don't know what to do but I can't walk away from this one, he has me wanting more, needing to see him, addicted to his smile. He is everything that I have always feared I would feel but now that I have it I can't let it go. He has opened my eyes and my heart to what life is really about. I hate it Lil, he literally makes me sick."

Lillian laughed, thinking that her friend was joking, and said, "yeah okay. Why did you really call me here?"

Her friend looked up from the swing where she sat and revealed that she was crying, another sight that Lillian had never seen, and she continued, "this isn't funny. My heart breaks when I think that someday I might lose him. I think about his heart moving on and I feel the need to vomit. I hate everything that is going on in my head right now. I am not this insecure idiot; I am strong and I don't need any man."

Marie put her head in her hands and shook her head with anger, "this is not something that I know what to do with. I feel crazy and I am so afraid of driving him away. I lose everything in my life that is important to me Lil, that's why I am so good at remaining detached. Please tell me how to stop feeling this way."

Lillian, in absolute awe of what she just heard, remained silent. Whatever she said, she knew that Marie would listen to her because of her current state; this was very stressful. She sat down in the swing beside her friend, cleared her throat, and said, "I am sorry to tell you this but I love you so I have to be honest with you." Lillian paused for a moment trying not to laugh and continued, "Mar, you are clearly in love. I would also like to take a moment to convince you that, believe it or not, this is not a terrible thing for you."

"I was hoping that wouldn't be your diagnosis", Marie said hanging her head extra low for effect.

"I am sorry but you have caught the incurable, disastrous, and always heartbreaking disease that we simpletons call love. How the hell did you let this happen?"

She shook her head seriously and said, "I don't know. One day we are going to dinner and the next night we got a little drunk on sake and I am telling him that we would have beautiful children."

"What!?" Lillian said eagerly.

"Exactly, this is brutal Lil. What the hell am I doing? This is not a part of my plan."

"Sometimes the best things that happen to us aren't part of the plan".

Marie shut her eyes and ran her hands through her long blonde hair, only getting caught for a moment in the knots. She took a deep breath in and let out, "he really is so wonderful. He is a good, honest, playful, wonderful man. He makes me doubt everything in my life and makes me consider how beautiful my future could be. I don't even want to fix him; he makes me want to fix myself."

"There you have it", Lillian laughed again admiring her friends confusion, "You are in love!" She stood from the swing on which she sat and reached her hand out, "let's go. We need champagne. This is a moment to celebrate; Marie the heartless wretch has fallen in love!"

Marie took Lillian's hand smiling at the inappropriate declaration. "Indeed I have", she said feeling everything and hating it.

The two practically skipped back to Connor and Lillian's apartment to break open the bottle of champagne that they had saved from their wedding for a special occasion; Lillian decided that this was the said occasion though her husband would not agree. When he got home and found them drunk and asleep on the couch.

Lillian swung for a few minutes more on the swing before she accepted it was time to go home and tell Connor about their creation. Lillian missed the deceased now more than ever because she knew that the news of a child would have made Marie cry; a truly real response that would be missed. Lillian left the playground and muttered, "you can never say that I didn't tell you first."

Katherine approached the stone that she bought to represent her daughter, though this was her first time visiting and laying her eyes on the engraved marble. She looked back at June who waved from across the cemetery as if to give her friend some courage. As she stood on top of the spot where Marie was buried, Katherine felt everything. She smiled and said "I am sober now. I have been sober for twenty-two days." She paused, expecting some sort of reply but she got none. "That also means that, even though you died so long ago, I have been trying to deal with your…with you dying, for twenty two days as well."

Katherine looked back and June was still wandering around the farthest section of the graveyard reading people's stones. She turned back to Marie and said, "I got you some flowers" she put down the bouquet of yellow roses that she had purchased. "I spoke with Tomas about how I have acted, well, I apologized for how I have acted. He says that he forgives me but I don't know why he would. He told me that Matt is moving away soon. Connor is having a dinner for the family to wish him farewell and…" she wiped the tears that so quickly streamed down her face, "…he called me to invite me for the dinner".

As she struggled into her jacket pocket she thought of why she was really here; Katherine pulled out a tissue and tried to flatten it out in order to make some use of it. She blew her nose and then continued, "I am here to thank you I think. Thank you for your letter. Thank you for taking care of your little brother for so many years when I couldn't." She reached back into her pocket to retrieve another tissue and she wiped her tears and then her nose. "I am so sorry that you couldn't live life anymore. James called me yesterday; he told me the truth. Do you know how sad it makes me that you couldn't come to me? My baby girl was dying and I couldn't even tell. I will be sorry for that forever and I will honour your hopes for me forever."

She stopped, thinking that she might be done, and said one last thing, "Before you left our family was pretty torn and I know that was largely my fault. It seems to me now that we might have a chance of pulling together again and I think that is because of you. Just thought you should know."

Katherine turned to walk away and stopped to the sight of a man standing only a few feet in front of her. She recognized his face but couldn't place him. Before she could say anything he said, "Hello Katherine".

"Have we met?" she asked.

"I am doctor Birmingham. I was Marie's psychiatrist." He said the words as if accepting blame and waited to receive her judgment of him.

Katherine smiled and put out her hand and as they shook she admired his blue eyes. "Yes, she talked about you a lot. You made quite an impression. Are you here for a visit?"

"I am actually. I haven't been here in some time so I thought I would stop by." Charles assessed that Katherine was not intoxicated which peeked his interest.

"Well I will let you get to it then. I should be going." She gave him a nod and a smile and started walking towards June who had been intently watching the two interact.

Charles returned the smile and turned towards the headstone. He didn't think about Marie. He did think about his ex-wife and how poorly she treated him. He also thought about the smile that he received from Katherine and how beautiful she was; he had never seen her smile nor had he ever heard of her being sober. He turned and jogged towards the two women who were walking out of the rod iron gate. "Wait!" he yelled out as he got closer to them. The two turned, surprised at his rapid approach.

When he reached them he took a minute to catch his breath and, when he realized how pathetic that was as he had only run about twenty meters, he looked at Katherine and asked her, "can I ask you a personal question?"

The two women looked at each other and June said "I will go wait in the car" and she left them alone.

"How personal is the question?" Katherine asked.

"How long have you been sober?"

Her eyes grew with shock, "How did you…?"

"Marie told me everything."

She nodded her head as if she had been betrayed but then quickly recognized that is was her who had betrayed herself, "Twenty-two days" she said looking to the ground.

Charles held his hand out and tipped her chin up, "that is really great for you" he said sincerely. She smiled because he had touched her chin and he knew that there was something there. "Would you like to have dinner with me when you reach thirty days?"

"Are you serious?"

"I am a shrink. We don't have the best sense of humor."

Katherine laughed and accepted his proposition by holding her hand out, "I would love to have dinner with you".

He took her hand and they stood shaking, looking at each other. Neither knowing what to do next; neither had been in this situation for decades. June watched and laughed at the awkwardness so she rolled down her car window and yelled to her friend, "We better get going now Kate!" The trance was broken and she kindly excused herself from his hand.

June watched as they exchanged numbers and Katherine, like a teenager, tried not to run in excitement back to the car. She got in and her face illuminated with a smile. June commented, "well this has been a big day for you. Not a lot of people get to clear their conscience with their daughter and get a date in the same day."

Katherine hit her friend's arm and said nothing because there was really nothing to say.

A waiter approached the table where James sat fidgeting with his tie. "Your wine sir?" he asked presenting an inexpensive bottle of Californian Cabernet Sauvignon.

"Yeah thanks," was the unenthusiastic reply.

The waiter poured the wine and looked around the room to check his other tables while James tasted the offering. He nodded in approval and the man standing over him asked, "could I get you anything else while you wait for your company sir?"

"I am fine thanks," he replied. As the waiter walked away to tend to another, James looked around the room and pulled again at his tie. He was not comfortable; he was too sober to be comfortable in this situation. He took in some wine. He held the glass by its stem and spun it around thinking. He thought about his day at work, what he would order for dinner and anything else that wasn't Marie. He quickly ran out of things to think about so he allowed a memory to haunt him for just a moment.

James took the empty bottle of wine off the table and into the kitchen where he opened a second. There had been an extended silence before he heard Marie say from the dining room table, "The thought of you being with someone else makes me sick."

"What was that?" he asked even though he clearly heard her.

"I see you having your first date and laughing at how charming she is; I dread you laughing. You will look into her eyes and love her without knowing her; you will see her naked when she looks casually away from you. You will feel her skin before you touch her; know her smell before you have her. It breaks my heart that you will be with another woman. It hurts me to leave you."

James came back into the room with a fresh bottle and poured into their two glasses. He sat and with a smile said, "I won't, I can't be with someone else."

"You will James, you are human and, more significantly, you are a man." She took a sip of the red zinfandel.

"Marie" he said offended.

"Shut up James. You are a healthy young man with a beautiful future; you won't give up women because I leave you. You will feel you should give up women for a while but you will love again. You are the nicest, most wonderful man I have ever known and it would be the world's loss if you didn't love again." Marie looked blankly into her glass of red wine as she spun it around in the glass.

"How can you say these things? You are my only love, the only one I will ever want." James reached across the table and put his hand on hers but she pulled away.

She felt a flash of guilt for distancing herself, this was a moment of weakness for her. "I wish you could see things the way I do. You will see women again after a while and then you will see one woman and then you will want again. I wish that you could know how my heart breaks at night when I watch you sleeping and I know that someone else will take my place. She will see you sleep and listen to you talk in your sleep; she will love you and have your love."

"Marie, stop", James said firmly.

"James, I am going to die" she aggressively rebutted.

"But you don't have to talk about it; we don't have to think about it. I will always love you; you are the love of my life."

Marie took the glass of wine back, gently thumped the glass on the table, looked directly into James' eyes and said, "I am not naVve; not a stupid girl....do you think I am dumb?"

"No", he replied.

"Do you think that a young, attractive, passionate man like yourself will remain single for long? Women will throw themselves at you because of your tragic past and your lost love. You will be a catch that no one will want to resist; women eat that shit up."

"Marie stop" James tried to hug her but she pulled away.

"You have helped me plan my funeral James; you have helped me look past my death and make decisions so that my loved ones won't have to. Well I have looked past me suffering, death and funeral and I am left wondering what the people I love will do. Will Mom still drink? Will Jones still be an artist? Will Connor and Lillian still listen to music? Will Jane be Jane? Will Chris still be a business man first? Will you still live your life to the fullest? The answer is yes; the answer will always be yes." James let a tear roll down his face but Marie continued, "I am going to die and nothing is really going to change. You all love me now but I will die, you will cry, and then life will continue as it has. Nothing will improve within my family. People will continue to do the things that make them happy and you, well, you will move on to someone new. You will get married and have babies and smile."

"I won't", he said passionately as he wept.

Marie remained stable and cold, "You will; James you should. You, before anyone else, need to be happy. You deserve so much more than I have ever been able to give you."

He wiped the stream of tears from his face with his sleeve "Marie, you taught me what happiness was." James then used his damp shirt sleeve to wipe his runny nose, "you taught me to think for myself and to be happy despite what people think of me or you or anything. You have been such a pain in my ass but I would never trade our time together for anything. You have been a wreck, mentally and physically, but you have made me so much stronger and braver just from knowing you. I will never know anyone who will take on so much pain to save others from it." He tried to hug her again because he needed strength and she gave into him and allowed him to embrace her.

On his shoulder she began to cry, "the physical pain is tiring but the pain I feel when I think of people moving on with their lives is unbearable."

"You will always be in our lives" he told her sincerely.

"I won't," Marie responded intelligently.

James held her away from him by the shoulders and looked her straight in the eyes and said, "Whether you believe it or not, it remains a fact, I will never forget you. If I have to I will read your depressing book over and over again until I kill myself"

She smiled hopelessly, "Well, thank you for saying so. In my fantasies I will picture you mourning me forever then."

"Perfect" James responded with satisfaction as if he had won a battle.

"Yeah, perfect," Marie said, warmly in his arms.

James came back to reality, when his table was approached again. "Hi James, sorry I am late" the red headed Rachel apologized.

"No problem," he said as he politely stood and they exchanged a kiss on the cheek. James gestured to her chair, "please sit down, I already ordered the wine because I wasn't sure if you were going to show," he gave a counterfeit laugh.

Rachel sat down and smiled as he poured her wine, "I wouldn't miss it for the world". She lifted her glass and held it out for a toast; when he conceded she spoke, "to a long time coming". She smiled confidently and took a sip of her wine while James deliberated on the toast she gave; he took a sip of his wine a little aggravated.

He didn't think this was a long time coming, he thought this was too soon. He only chose Rachel because he knew her before and thought there would be some comfort in that. As she read the menu he drank his wine and watched her. He thought her smile was shallow because it never left her face; a smile was a gift to someone who earned it. She had her hair up off of her neck but she had lacked the creativity to do anything but put it in a ponytail. Her freckles would have been cuter had she not smeared makeup all over them. Her lipstick seemed wrong for her though James couldn't put his finger on why and her eye makeup looked like she put it on yesterday and it smeared all over the place as she slept.

She looked up from the menu and noticed James admiring her. "Well, since you are the chef here why don't you order for me? I don't really like garlic or onions very much but anything else is usually okay."

James laughed and replied bitterly, "well since you don't like two of the most wonderful ingredients in the world then why don't you just pick apart the menu yourself and request what you think you'll like?"

Rachel stared at him not quite sure how to respond. He could see her confusion and he recognized what he was doing. "I am sorry. I didn't mean to sound like an asshole. This is very hard for me and I am taking my frustrations out on you. I will pick something for you to eat that will be delicious."

"Thank you," she replied, "I am just going to run to the bathroom, I will be right back." She gripped her purse and as she walked through the restaurant every man with eyes watched with enjoyment as she passed.

"I must be crazy" James said out loud as he ran his fingers through his hair. He decided to try and make this night work out. It would be stupid of him not to enjoy someone who has been throwing herself at him for years.

He ordered her dinner while she was gone and when she returned he made every effort to have a nice dinner. The food was great and she enjoyed his choices. They drank two bottles of wine and flirted over every glass. He slowly was able to see her physical beauty through the haze of guilt that followed him everywhere as the liquor released him. She was a nice girl; a nice and beautiful girl who was interested in him.

It came time for dessert and they shared a mousse; quite a sexual gesture he decided. She had a specialty coffee and he enjoyed a few ounces of ice wine. And the moment came where James knew absolutely that he could have all of her tonight if he so chose. She excused herself and as she walked back to the washroom he liked the way he could see through her dress when the light hit it a certain way.

He finished his ice wine as he waited and he realized how drunk he was. He laughed at how silly this night was; him being on a date and finally planning on having sex. He tried not to think of Marie; now was not the time for reminiscing. Despite his best efforts he couldn't forget their first time together.

Naked bodies inches from each other, they lay peacefully admiring the intricacies of the other's face. She ran her left hand down the side of his face because she needed to touch him, to feel what she had been admiring.

When they made eye contact the two paused, she held her breath. When he watched her uncomfortably shut her eyes and tilt her head away from him shyly, he smiled and tapped her chin lightly with his hand to guide her back towards him. Her face returned but her eyes were fixed on his lips. They kissed. It was a soft kiss that confirmed that they were equally vulnerable.

He held her close like she wanted to be held, and perfectly so. Her head tucked in between his chin and his chest, she closed her eyes and took in a deep breath; she was completely taken by him. Her mind returned and she came to terms with the fact that she was in love. Upon this realization she felt equally ecstatic and nauseous, liberated and scared; love was not something that she usually allowed. Love makes you weak, makes you stupid and, therefore, you end up hurt. He let out a satisfied moan as he tightened his squeeze on her and she lost her train of thought.

She ran her fingers down his torso, pausing for a second to tease his nipple. He pretended to be unaffected by her wandering hands but she knew better. She pulled her head from his chest to look at his face. He grinned as if to challenge her and she considered the competition. She delicately placed her head back on his chest and took a moment to consider her strength and the effort she would have to put in to win at this game.

She looked him in the eyes and said "thank you".

"For what" he asked.

"For everything" she replied before she kissed him semi passionately with all the affection that she could.

She pulled away but he pulled her back and kissed her harder. He kissed her harder because he cared so much about her but she didn't take it that way. She wanted to be with him. She wrapped her legs tightly around him to force him closer. Neither of them, despite exhaustion, could pass up the chance to be together, to feel each other.

They both lay on their sides, simultaneously kissing and plotting their plan of attack. He knew that he was fatigued and couldn't last all night so he became the aggressor. He rolled her on to her back and rested some of his weight on her body. He didn't attempt to start anything without her persuasion though; she persuaded him.

Her mouth was just above his shoulder; he could hear her enjoy him or feel her bite down when she held back. Her hands rolled up and down his back, pausing at times to grip tightly at moments that she couldn't hide her pleasure. He concentrated on lasting though she was making it difficult. Her hips forced towards him and he slowed down. She pulled him towards her demanding him to resume. He did what she wanted. Her hands made their way down to his lower back and she pulled him into her. He did what she wanted. She said his name. Their bodies were still pressing tightly against each other. He forgot why he was fighting it. They made eye contact. Her eyes closed and her mouth opened, she was holding back because she knew he was watching. He finished shortly thereafter because he was watching.

She felt his weight become heavier on her chest. He remained on her as he caught his breath and gathered enough energy to move. She hugged him tightly in appreciation and let out a chuckle as she tends to do because she lacks the ability to hold her satisfaction in.

He lifted his head and kissed her softly as he had the last time they were in such a situation. They both smiled and he embraced her before he excused himself. They returned to their position on their sides where they laid comfortably, admiring the intricacies of the other's face. He told her that she was beautiful and she awkwardly assured him that he was beautiful too. He denied what his mind was trying to justify. She remained ecstatic and nauseous.

Things would have been better for them if they both knew that the other was feeling the exact same way. Sadly though, they were going to quietly hide their love away until it was safe. Tonight though, they comfortably fell asleep in each other's arms feeling nothing short of perfect contentment.

James shook the memory away; he was moving on from that now.

When Rachel returned to the table she reached across the table to hold his hand. James saw her moving in and his confidence went through the roof. She stroked his hand delicately making chills go down his spine and as fast she affected him, he ripped his hand away from hers.

"What's wrong?" Rachel asked kindly.

"This is wrong. I can't do this to you," he said.

"Can't do what?" she wondered.

"I am in love with her still and I don't think it is okay for me to sleep with you just to relieve myself."

Rachel sat a little taken back. "You wouldn't be relieving yourself; you would be opening yourself up to something more. This is hard for you, I know, but it is okay that you still love her and that you are moving on with me."

"Would it be okay if I was still in love with someone who was breathing?" he asked hopefully.

"Well, no, but that is different. If you were in love with someone else who was alive, why would you want to be with me?"

"That is what I thought. I don't see anything in you that would lead to a real relationship between us so I don't think that I can waste either of our time."

"Since when is sex a waste of time?" She asked offensively.

James paused before his reply because he had many answers for her. The one that surfaced first was the one he told her, "Having sex with other people after you have had sex with the love of your life is like a masturbating. It gets the job done but you are left wishing you had the real thing."

"Wow that was really deep James. Why don't you call me tomorrow when you sober up? Our next date is not going to involve alcohol." Rachel got up from the table and leaned over to kiss him on the cheek. He allowed it.

"There won't be another date Rachel. But thank you for tonight, I needed to know."

"You'll call me, trust me," she replied as she strutted away. James admired her as she left but his admiration was that she woke him up. He didn't need to pine over the dead anymore. He needed to find someone that would make him happy like Marie once did; not to replace her but to compliment her. Someone with whom he could create a life that included a memory.

When Connor and Lillian approached Matthew and Josie's house, Jones sat on the worn steps shaking his head at something Tomas had told him. Lillian saw that there was something to be said without her present so she hugged Tomas hello and gave Jones a wave of recognition before she went into the house. Jones looked up at his brother who stood over him and he chuckled, "you aren't going to believe this", he said with a smile.

Connor looked to his eldest brother and then his youngest, before daring to say, "looks like something entertaining."

Tomas, who didn't think it was very funny at all replied, "mom is coming for dinner".

"And apparently she is sober now", Jones added as if it were all a joke.

"She IS sober now", Tomas said protectively. He looked over to Connor and asserted again, "she is sober now".

"How did this happen?" Connor asked as if some sort of tragedy had occurred.

"Which thing? Her sobering up or her getting an invite to dinner?" Jones asked sarcastically.

Connor looked up at his elder brother and shook his head at him, "the sobering part."

"I think it was a combination of June and Marie" Tomas shrugged, "but I don't really know for sure".

Before they could continue, Lillian, very ungracefully, opened the door in a rush and as soon as she and Connor made eye contact he said "I already know". As if she was sneaking away from someone, she shut the door behind her and she approached the trio of brothers.

"So you know your mom is coming?"

"Yep."

"I have more." She confessed deviously, "Josie is upstairs crying because your brother is throwing himself this going away party as if it is a celebration."

Jones shook his head again and blurted, "it isn't surprising that his complete selfishness is making another person cry, I will go in and talk to him again. Let's see if I can make him even remotely aware of what he is doing." He got up and went into the house like a hero goes off to war, on a mission and detached from any other focus.

Lillian continued, "and Connor, he didn't invite James. I know that you two had talked about it but I didn't want you to find out that he wasn't coming when we were sitting down to eat." Connor didn't say anything he just nodded and went inside to talk to Matthew much like Jones had done seconds before. She laughed at the dramatic exit and turned to Tomas, "how are you doing little brother?" she asked him, who had been standing obediently without saying a word.

"I got accepted into university for the fall" he said meekly.

Lillian beamed a smile and wrapped her arms around him, "I am so proud of you, that's amazing, I didn't even know that you had applied". She put her hands on his shoulders, looking straight at him, which always made him feel uncomfortable, and she continued, "I can't believe how amazing you are considering your circumstances. Don't get me wrong, I know that you are all a little fucked up, but you have had the worst of everything and yet you are the most together. Good for you Tommy."

He smiled because he appreciated her but he replied. "Marie had it the most together of us all. I just learned from her."

She smiled back and said enthusiastically, "well as long as you don't go jumping off of any cliffs". There was silence before they shared a sad glance and she took him by the hand and walked him inside to face the music.

As they entered, Matthew passed them and said hello before he head up the stairs to talk to Josie. Lillian could see that Jones had been effective. She and Tomas went into the kitchen to see that Jones and Connor had taken over dinner. "Lil, would you please call James and invite him for a family dinner. Tell him it is a going away party for Matt and that should be incentive enough for him to come." Jones and Tomas laughed because they knew the truth in his statement. Lillian went to make the call and left the brothers alone again. Tomas knew that he wouldn't be much use in the kitchen so he poured himself some wine and pulled up a stool to the island hoping that someone would talk to him.

"So Tommy, tell me about Katherine being sober" Jones said as he stirred the sauce he was working on.

The question made him feel uncomfortable but he knew that both people in the room were interested in his answer. "She is like she was before. She is even nicer now though because she feels really bad for everything. Mom has turned into a person that can cook and clean and feel and talk; it's great. She is very nervous about seeing you both tonight. Matthew went to see her when I told him that she was better; he agrees that she really is better." Tomas stopped to see if there was any commentary; there was none, so he continued. "She has been on a date with a man. I think that helps a lot. She smiles now; she says nice things; there is less breakage around the house." He smiled to ensure his positive outlook on the new situation.

Connor stopped chopping, "that's good Tom, that's really good for her. It's good for you too."

"That's good for her?" Jones questioned sarcastically. "Just because she has spent a little while without a bottle stuffed in her mouth doesn't make everything go away".

"Is it really worth it to you?" Connor asked. "Wouldn't it be easier to let go and get over it?"

Jones, holding a lot of childhood angst, felt hurt that his little brother could so easily forgive her and, so, he excused himself, "I am going out for a smoke, Tommy, come here and stir this...make sure you don't let it burn" Jones grabbed his cigarettes from his jacket pocket and went to the front porch, slamming the door behind him.

Connor instinctually wanted to protect his little brother, "Don't worry about him Tom, he will get over it. I am glad to hear that things are better at home. I really am."

Lillian came back in the kitchen before he could continue. "I left a message", she said knowing that Connor was about to ask the question. She was lying; James told her that it would be too hard for him to come to a family dinner uniting everyone for the first time. Marie had tried for years to bring everyone together again but was never successful, except in the case of her funeral.

"There is wine there on the counter", Tomas told her.

"No wine for me tonight Tom, but thanks for letting me know."

"What do you mean no wine? That would be like Marie saying no to a glass of wine." He laughed before he sorted out what that had to mean. He had a blank look on his face but them smiled and turned to her, "are you?"

Lillian nodded happily and Tomas abandoned the sauce that he promised to protect to go over and hug his sister in law, and he turned to Connor to congratulate him as well. Tomas joked, "Matt is going to be so pissed that your news is going to ruin his day in the spotlight."

Connor laughed and said, "I don't think I care much to be honest."

"Fair enough" Tomas said beaming, "I don't care either". He was lying though; he very much feared what Matthew's reaction would be and how it would shape the evening. He thought not to reveal such fears to Connor at this moment; this was happy time. Everyone smiled and it was nice. Tomas enjoyed being part of this, part of something.

The moment wasn't long enjoyed before Matthew left his weeping wife upstairs and returned to a kitchen full of smiling faces which irritated him. "What are you guys talking about?" he asked.

Connor laughed, touched his shoulder and said, "nothing bro, just making some inappropriate jokes."

Matthew smiled "oh yeah? Fill me in, I am always up for a good joke."

Lillian took a guess that her husband had no ability to tell a dirty joke and no intention to tell the truth so she chimed in, "I would really rather not hear that one again. It was neither funny nor dirty."

"Okay, no problem", Matthew said, not wanting to irritate another woman this day. "Are you stirring that?" he asked Connor, not overly confident in his ability to make a béarnaise sauce."

Connor smiled patiently and chose his words wisely, "Go upstairs and see if you can coax your wife downstairs for dinner. I am fine with the sauce. It would be nice to spend some time with everyone together as a family tonight. Mom will be here soon and it would be best if her first dinner with us in years isn't as dramatic and evasive as our childhood."

Matthew was angry with his brother for eluding to his family unit as dramatic but he said nothing. He turned away from the responsibility of dinner and he returned to his family commitments for the moment.

He wasn't out of the kitchen for more than a minute before the front door opened and the usually over confident and strong eldest sibling hopped through the opening and within seconds he nervously announced that his mother was walking up the street. Then he excused himself to the washroom with no intent to return. Tomas knew that it would be him to meet her at the door because all of the others, whom he had admired for their strength since he was born, had been completely paralyzed with fear. Even Lillian remained wary in the kitchen with Connor and Jones.

Katherine knocked once before Tomas swung open the door to greet her. His mother had her hair done that day and she had spent some time over applying her makeup in order to make a good impression. She was carrying a cloth bag full of what looked like books and a bottle of non alcoholic wine; she had parted with liquor but not the satisfaction and habit of lifting a glass to her mouth. Tomas noticed that she was wearing new clothes as well and that her lipstick was too dark for her face, "you look nice", he said.

"Thank you, it's all old stuff I just found in my closet" she said looking down at herself and lying through her teeth.

Tomas' heart broke for her but he kept up the façade, "well you make those old clothes look good".

Katherine, shaking as she did when she was going through withdrawal, asked her youngest son, despite how hard she resisted, "is everyone here? Do they know I am here?"

Tomas, again unable to speak the truth, answered "they are in the kitchen. Jones is having the hardest time with this so don't push it too hard or fast okay?"

Katherine smiled and asked where the kitchen was. He pointed and she slowly crept in. Lillian, Connor and Jones were desperately silent awaiting her entrance; a form of torture that brought two of them back to their childhood.

When she came around the corner, not one of them faced her, they all acted out a very important thing that they needed to be doing. There was a possibility that a mother would have noticed the blatant disregard for her presence but, luckily, Katherine was fairly new to sobriety and awareness. She didn't have the courage to announce herself but she approached Lillian and when she turned to face her mother in law, they embraced. Lillian turned it on, "how are you? Tommy tells us that you are getting yourself together!"

"That is the blunt way of saying it," Katherine said a little shocked, "but I am sorting myself out."

"What does sorting yourself out mean?" Jones asked bitterly as he turned from his very important task.

"You know what it means Jonsey"

"Please don't call me that. I am too old to hear that name now." He turned back to his sauce that had been done for five minutes and he stirred it diligently.

Katherine turned to Connor, "are you still pretty angry with me too Con?"

Connor turned to his mother and wife and looked to Lillian for the strength that she always gave him. She smiled to him and he slowly approached the two women. His mother held her breath knowing how difficult this was for him, and she said "I know how hard this is for you."

"No you don't", Lillian said protectively.

"Maybe not", the matriarch replied. Katherine held out her hand as if they were two businessmen meeting for the first time, "I am a new woman and I would appreciate it if you would get to know me".

Connor had always longed for his mother's return into his life but he didn't want to seem to desperate for it. He played it cool, took her hand and shook it and said, "It is bad business to forget about the past because it is always a good indicator of the future."

She nodded because she agreed with him, "I hope that the future will be no indicator of the past. I think that, in our case that would be best."

He nodded in agreement and their hands fell from each other and he returned to his culinary tasks. Jones remained statuesque.

Katherine looked around and asked, "Where's my granddaughter?"

"They are upstairs" Lillian answered, "you should go up and see them, they will be happy that you are here".

"Thank you, I will come back down in a few minutes so we can catch up."

Jones shot out sarcastically, "we can't wait".

Katherine left, seemingly unaffected by the comment, and Lillian started to set the table. She seemed to realize that dinner had been ready for the past fifteen minutes when the two chefs in the kitchen were oblivious; she dare not say a word about it. It did come together in a short time with her influence.

***

Dinner was a little over cooked considering the talent in charge but the diners didn't mind as they knew that there was a lot on everyone's mind. They ate almost in pure silence aside from some courtesy questions like 'how did you make this sauce' or 'could you pass the salt please'. Josie wouldn't lift her head from her plate; she just stared right at it refusing to pretend that this was okay. Amelie was sleeping quietly upstairs and everyone else wished to be somewhere else.

Lillian decided to be the one to make the first move. She cleared her throat and said to her silent company, "So, I would like to make a toast to Tomas who will be attending University next year."

Everyone raised their glasses and unanimously congratulated Tomas on his success; half of them meant it. Lillian continued, "I would also like to congratulate Katherine on being a grandmother for the second time".

Connor looked to his wife with disbelief of what she had just announced but he couldn't help himself but to smile. Katherine stood up in disbelief and approached the two of them to hug them and congratulate them with joyous tears. Josie even got up to embrace her sister in law with joy. Everyone was smiling and talking and ignoring the food in front of them at this point; everyone but Matthew who continued to eat as if nothing had been said. Jones noticed his little brother's lack of enthusiasm and said with warning in his voice, "Matt, did you hear that? Connor and Lil are having a baby."

"Yeah I heard", he replied bitterly.

Jones grew even more disappointed in his brother's selfishness, "Maybe you should go up and check on Amelie while we celebrate."

Matt looked up to his brother towering over him aggressively and he nodded and left the room with barely anyone noticing. Before anyone could see a missing brother Lillian continued, "and Katherine has an announcement to make". Everyone was silent and Lillian turned to Katherine for her to take the floor. She very meekly began but no one could hear her so she tried to raise her voice like a bartender trying to speak over the music.

"I want to thank you all for inviting me tonight. I know how hard it must be to accept me into your lives again; I don't expect it to be immediate or inevitable, I just hope that it might be a consideration. I especially wanted to thank Matty for coming to my house and encouraging me to come tonight; where is Matt?" She looked around but almost immediately moved on to her next thought, "I really wanted everyone to know that Marie's book will be in book stores next week. I brought a few copies that the publishing company sent me in case anyone wants it before it comes out. I read it myself; it is interesting to read words that she wrote." Katherine lowered her head to hide her welling eyes. Josie went to her and rubbed her back as she took a seat.

At this point everyone sat back down because their excitement had turned to remorse. Almost everyone was thinking about the last time she sat at this table with them and announced that her book was going to be published; that was the week before she died.

Jones was the first to say something, "I was jealous that night when she said that her book was being published. I was so envious that she was so successful at her age and I had accomplished nothing. I know that is all garbage now and I know I don't really feel that way but it kills me that she died and her last memory of me was that I brushed off the importance of her accomplishment." He gestured to Josie to ask permission to smoke inside and she nodded in approval.

"It's funny, I call that her 'last supper'" Lillian said smiling ironically as any good pagan making a Christian reference would.

"What last supper?" Katherine asked anxiously.

Tomas answered so others wouldn't have to explain why she wasn't invited to the last family event that her daughter was alive for, "we had a dinner when Marie asked us all together to tell us some news. She told us about her book being taken on by a publisher but she was really saying goodbye to us; just none of us knew that at the time."

Katherine's tears of joy turned into tears of regret. She wiped her face shamefully and asked, "what did she say?"

Everyone else in the room exchanged looks because they all knew that this was a topic best avoided. She persisted with a louder voice, more difficult to ignore, "what did she say?"

They each took a turn explaining to her the last night they spent with Marie over wine and dinner. The only person who saw Marie after the dinner was Lillian on the day she died, but she dare not reveal that or she would have to betray her friend's confidence. Everyone sat down around the table and took turns explaining that night to Katherine.

Marie and James had brought over hundreds of dollars in food, champagne and fine wine. James had prepared the dinner with the boys, all getting drunk and thoroughly enjoying the experience. Marie had spent the evening hugging and kissing her niece and conversing with Lillian and Josie about nothing much in particular. The women had inquired about her weight loss and pale complexion but that was easily explained when she joked about taking up the life of a vampire and then following up with the excuse that she had pneumonia for a few weeks but that she was on the upside of it now. Her brothers would rarely notice such physical attributes in their sister as she had always been weak and sick in childhood and into her adult life.

After dinner had been served and Connor joked about her winning the lottery instead of asking why she had spent so much money on the evening because he feared the answer. Marie sat in her place and raised her glass to make a toast. Everyone was curious so they were attentive to her action; she couldn't hold her glass up long so she stood instead.

She began, "I wanted to thank Matt for letting me use his house for a dinner party. I also wanted to thank all of my brothers for taking time out of their busy lives to meet in one place for the first time since we were children. I know that we never get together anymore but I just feel like we should because, despite our parents, we all love each other and we are all functional for the most part." She smiled when she heard some chuckles from her audience.

She continued, but her smile faded with her energy, "I brought you all here to tell you something very important to me. It may not matter to all of you but you need to try and understand that this is everything to me and I need you to pretend to care if you can't do it sincerely. I have tried my whole life to be something to all of you. I have tried very hard to be a good sister, a good friend and a good woman." James smiled at her because he didn't have a clue where she was going with this and he was a little nervous about it.

She smiled back at him, and kept talking to their company, "I love all of you so much and I want to share everything with all of you; I want to share every tragedy, every happiness, every accomplishment, and I hope you all feel the same."

"What's going on?" Lillian asked nervously.

Marie smiled with excitement, "My book is being published".

The sound of everyone getting excited and talking at the same time overcame the room. It was like chatter, where no one could really understand anything other than what they were saying. After a few minutes Matthew interrupted the talking, "whoa, how could you publish a book that none of us have read?"

Marie smiled, "Samson and James have read it. Other than them, none of you would have given me constructive criticism; not that James gave me any criticism at all."

"Well what's it about?" asked Connor.

There was no reply from the author as she sat back down.

James could see that she was nervous to talk about her exploit in front of the only people whose opinions mattered. He answered for her, "It is about two people who don't know how to be happy and they rely on each other to find meaning in their lives."

Marie added, "It's about watching someone die and what they care to share with the world before they leave."

No one said a word they just made faces and thought about it. "I like it" Lillian chimed in and Connor quickly followed suit. Within a minute everyone seemed to be on board with the idea. They all toasted with Champagne and gave many more congratulations.

"When do we get to read it?" Josie asked.

Marie's face revealed that she didn't know the answer, "I don't think I will have much control over that to be honest".

She and James excused themselves not long after her announcement because she was tired. Everyone questioned why she would leave and why she wasn't drinking but everyone came to their own conclusions; none of which were even remotely accurate.

When they finished explaining that night to Katherine she sat still, without tears, without expression, "I guess I don't blame you for not inviting me, no one knew. I would have ruined it I bet by saying something inappropriate".

"We didn't know it was her last supper", Jones said honestly.

Katherine sat reflecting on what she had lost in her drunken haze. Her company thought better of interrupting her thought process so they slowly moved out of the dining room and into the living room to give her some time alone.

Jones was the first to ask, "so who will get the money from her book?"

Lillian knew the answer, "James gets everything".

"Good" said Connor, "It is best to go to him rather than her. She doesn't need any encouragement to get back on the wagon."

Tomas had an unanswered question himself, "so was it an accident?"

"Was what an accident", Josie asked innocently.

Matthew entered the room as he came down from Amelie's room, "he is asking if Marie's death was an accident or not. Whether or not she jumped or fell."

Connor turned with a fraction of hope for his brother, "what do you think Matt?"

Matthew destroyed that hope in a few sentences, "what do I think Connor? I think that she was so desperate for attention that she jumped off a cliff. I think that even though years have passed she is still stealing attention away with her one selfish act. I think that you are all so consumed with her stupid death that you don't realize that I will be leaving too in a couple of days. How could you think of anything else though, after all of this shit coming out tonight? Will everyone miss me this much that they will sulk in a room thinking of the good times?"

Jones laughed obnoxiously and stood so that he could grab his brother's shirt and lift him slightly to his level, "you are choosing to leave us brother. You are abandoning your family for your own selfish reasons."

Matthew ripped away from his brother's grip, and looked angrily into his eyes, "she chose to leave too, don't forget. She abandoned all of us because it was easier than living. And you know what…I would have rather watched her die from cancer than lose her the way we did. She had no right to take that away from us." His rage began to reveal itself in his tears, "she chose to leave and never come back and you treat her like she was a martyr; why can't I decide my own life? Why can't I pursue the life that I want?" He sat down on his couch and not one person went to comfort him.

Katherine came in because she heard someone raising their voice and Matthew left to go upstairs; Josie followed him like a good wife would.

Everyone made themselves comfortable in the living room while Lillian and Katherine went to clear the table and get the coffee and dessert ready.

The boys began a conversation about video games and the ladies continued to focus on their lost company. As Katherine brought in the plates and awkwardly piled them into the sink without clearing them of leftover food she said quietly, "I hear from Tomas that James has started dating again".

Lillian nodded. "He has been on a date or two. He isn't enjoying it though Katherine, he is just trying to live his life despite the pain."

"He is moving pretty fast don't you think?" She asked feeling as if he was cheating on them all. "I just never thought that he would move on so easily."

"You have to know that it is as hard for him as it is for all of us; probably harder for him actually because she was all he had."

Katherine shook her head because it was difficult for her to accept and the two women gathered the coffee cups together and took them into the boys. As they came into the room Connor asked his mother, "did you get a letter mom?"

She nodded and looked around the room, "who else did?"

Lillian chimed in, "Connor and I got one".

Jones explained that he didn't get a letter but Marie sent him Matthew's letter with the direction to give it to him when he got nicer. "So it might be a while" he added.

They all looked to Tomas who nodded to indicate that he had also received a letter. When it was established that she had something to tell each of them, no one wanted to know what it was for anyone else. They remained hushed until Lillian changed the subject by asking Katherine about her new beau.

The rest of the evening was spent painting broad strokes of their lives to give their mother a vague idea of what had been happening over the years that she had lost. Jones managed to smile at her at least twice and Matthew ended up joining his family for the conversation without so much as one selfish outburst. Though there was much that remained unsaid; this was a night to forget about the things that hurt and to remember everything else.

Jane was walking through the mall on her lunch break trying to pass the time. She wandered past the usual stores but nothing in particular caught her eye. Her thoughts were continually ending back at memories of Marie. It was close to the anniversary of her friend's death but she had no way of knowing for sure which day it was and she certainly wasn't going to call Katherine to ask.

As she passed the book shop it occurred to her to check the shelves. Jane had not yet gathered the strength to read it and remained uncertain whether she ever would. She searched through the many titles and stopped suddenly; it was there. She stared at the spine for some time before picking it out from the shelf.

Jane opened the book to the dedication which read: *When one door closes another door opens; but we so often look so long and so regretfully upon the closed door, that we do not see the ones that open for us. – Alexander Graham Bell*

She then flipped through to the center pages. She read a few lines and flipped to the last page.

"*The thing about loss is that you can't make sense of it. You go through all the stages and when you reach the end, which is supposed to be acceptance, you still only feel loss. How can you accept something that you don't understand? How can you claim to be at ease when you never will be again? For those who can, I feel sorry for you; you are lying to yourself.*

The thing about loss is that it is a terrible, excruciating experience and no one should ever have to face it. The more infuriating thing about it is that everyone does, at one point or another, have to face it. Because of this inevitability, one can only mourn and feel sorry for them self for so long. You have to realize that it is yourself that you are crying for and not them. You are here in a world that you knew with them and they are gone. One can only cry so many selfish tears.

I suppose there is a point to this. Everyone expresses death in a different way from the person before him. This is my expression. Life is here for us to enjoy until it's gone and after that we stay alive through the memory of others. Our reaction to a loss is to cry, to mourn. After a time we need to persevere and move on to enjoy what life that we have left. After a time we need to know that they are gone. A tragedy, especially those that come unannounced, forces maturity, strength and growth. There will always be pain that reminds you of how much you loved; that's okay. Your pain is a monument to the life that once was; if no one feels the loss, what does that say about the life?"

Jane closed the book and placed it back on the shelf. She looked at the spine again as she contemplated and, despite the urge to walk away; she pulled the book from its shelf and bought it. When she went home that evening, she placed it on her fireplace where it sat for months before she thought to pick it up again.

Marie gripped on as hard as she could but she knew she didn't have the strength to do it for very long. She took a minute to catch her breath before the tears started streaming down her face. "I can't die like this" she said to herself, "I can't die like this, I can't die like this, I can't die like this."

She closed her eyes to regain some calm and maintain a clear mind. She could barely move without losing her grip so she settled for her limited ability to briefly turn her head from side to side in order to find a way back up to the safer spot on the cliff where she had stood moments ago.

Marie noticed a small step up about a meter away to her right. She couldn't look down to her feet because she would have to put too much distance between her and the rock that was holding her there so she shed a tear and had to trust that she would make it over there on the ledge that she so trusted at this moment.

She shuffled her feet very cautiously towards the hopefully stable step up from her current standing.

Her right foot slipped on some rock. She tightened up with fear as the stones tumbled down, bouncing off of the rough wall. She regained her footing and kept moving because she could feel her weakness overtaking her will.

When Marie reached the step that she saw as her savior this day, she tested it with her right foot and, when she approved of its safety, she put her weight on it. She was raised up high enough to reach out for a bush. She got the plant in her hand and tested its strength and then she held on as tight as she could and she did nothing. "Please give me strength to perform this one task", she said to herself like a coach gives a pep talk to a team that can't win.

She looked at the plant and smiled to give it the strength to hold her. When she realized how silly she was being, she let out a ghastly moan scream and used all of her strength to lift herself back onto the cliff.

She was successful; though there was blood. When she got over the edge and the majority of her weight was on the good side of the rocky rim, she crawled as fast as she could away from the plummet. She sat against her white bloomed tree and she cried. Her wounds were staining her virgin dress while she was trying to deal with the shock of what just happened.

She had no phone to call anyone. She didn't know what she would say if she did call. She wept some more, "that was so close" she whined to herself.

When she realized the ridiculousness of her current situation she attempted to stand, though, she had done some damage to her legs and they were still shaking. When she stood up, she noticed the absolute mess that she had made of her dress, staining it with blood and dirt. "This is not as I planned it", she said to herself with the tears slowing "but it doesn't really change anything".

She raised her head and looked again over the city where she was born. As she admired the beauty of the trees moving in the spring breeze she took a few steps further back away from the edge that almost took her prematurely.

Marie shut her eyes and she felt her final tears slowly roll down her face and stop at her chin; they lingered for a moment before they jumped. She smiled as the breeze swept through her hair and she could feel it dancing around her; *a very romantic goodbye*, she thought.

Her eyes opened, her smile faded, and she looked towards the sky for her very last secret request for courage. It was granted to her.

She looked to the cliff's edge and, though it seemed to be in slow motion, she ran as fast as she could towards it with no regrets. She approached the end of her road and she hurled herself over the ledge that she had always feared. The fall made her feel like a bird; much like she had expected. Then she felt nothing; a freedom that she had longed for her entire life.

CPSIA information can be obtained at www.ICGtesting.com
Printed in the USA
268718BV00003B/5/P